The Story of Prince
An Enthralling Book U
Remarkable Life

"Everyone of us needs to show how much we care for each other and, in the process, care for ourselves"

- Lady Diana Spencer -

By Holly S Calloway

Legal Notice:

Disclaimer Notice:

TABLE OF CONTENTS

INTRODUCTION

It is pointless to attempt to define Princess Diana using broad generalizations. Others who judge her only on her philanthropic efforts are as biased as others who depict her as a hungry soul who yearned in vain for real love. Though remembering Diana for the immense humanitarian impact she had on the world is a nice thought, defining her purely on those efforts is unrealistic. The princess was a mysterious lady who led a complicated existence.

What is known is that Diana's youth influenced all that came after. Her parents adored her, but they were sometimes distant and emotionally unavailable. She was mothered and fathered by a series of caring nannies, the majority of whom she liked, but none of whom could ever replace the strong emotional relationship established by truly committed and adoring parents.

Diana's compassionate nature can also be explained by the seeds she planted early in life. She felt entitled to the collection of fluffy critters she had moth-ered as a child. Diana acquired a profound empathy for the weak and less fortunate at a young age. She recognized that, just as she needed someone to look after her, those helpless animals needed others to look after them, and she did it with all the energy and passion she could muster.

Di-ana's two most motivating impulses in life were her desire to reclaim love lost in her formative years and her innate sentiments for others in need. Despite her desire for attention and appreciation, her lack of confidence led to poor academic and early job-related performance. She was a fantastic princess because talking with people, many of whom were very impoverished and sick, was a perfect match for her strengths. Indeed, her concern for others helped her to become one of history's most revered women.

Nonetheless, her great desire to find the love and affection she got from people all around the world would haunt her until her terrible death. Though her affections for Prince Charles began as a youthful crush, there is no doubt that by the time they married in 1981, they had evolved into genuine love. Despite the bride and groom's emotional struggle, the wedding offered a real-life fairy tale for the globe. Millions of people across the world tuned in to see Diana and Charles enter into a sacred bond, but also to see a nation captivated by the proceedings. The princess's extraordinary beauty created the groundwork for the adulation she would receive throughout her travels.

But, regrettably, her passion for Charles waned as the years passed and she realized it would never be returned. His ongoing affair with Camilla Parker Bowles hindered him from making a commitment to Diana and prevented her from giving him her undivided attention. Her emotional relationship to her marriage faded as she matured emotionally and sexually in her mid-twenties. Diana began looking for a happy relationship elsewhere after realizing he was no longer faithful to her.

Princess Diana's adult life was marked by intelligence and goodness, which manifested itself in her professional activity. Her self-assurance rose as it became clear early in her marriage that she was considerably more popular than her husband, which was a source of considerable humiliation for him. As she approached her late twenties, she demonstrated a passion and authenticity unrivaled by any other star of her generation. Her subsequent divorce from Charles gave her the freedom to choose the pet charities that most touched her heart—always those that demanded the most emotional and physical sacrifices.

Others in her position may have chosen to devote their time and energy to noncontroversial problems or those that did not concern the world's poorest countries or people. Diana, on the other hand, was drawn to people who were crying for aid. She cared for the homeless, the hungry, the AIDS children, battered women, and the indigent, and she pushed to have anti landmines banned. Her natural affinity for child care did not require development; it was a natural extension of her childhood. Diana was caring for individuals she perceived to be in need of her love and attention, just as she had done with her dogs decades before. Every moment, every hug, every glance demonstrated the power of her persuasion, from the moment an African child inquired whether she was an angel to the moment she fearlessly went through a minefield. Critics said that it was all a sham, but anyone who had been touched by the princess strongly disagreed. And the attention Diana brought to these concerns made a significant effect in the lives of millions of people. After all, it was only after her travels to those affected by anti landmines in Africa, Asia, and Europe that 122 countries decided to ban them.

A person's greatness is measured throughout time by what they accomplish for people with whom they share the globe. Diana, like the most revered personalities in history, struggled with personal issues and flaws. Her contributions to the world, however, will be remembered for a long time. The same heart that craved love so intensely that it clouded her judgment was also used to help the defenseless and provide hope to the despairing, to feed the hungry, and to cast a light on those who lived in darkness.

Diana remains a beacon for the globe, particularly for those with the means to improve the lives of the poor millions. To be sure, financial contributions are vital in the fights against hunger, homelessness, and disease. However, the time and desire to put a famous face on such challenges inspires others to make a difference. Putting a focus on a much-needed humanitarian effort is just as vital as pouring money at it, because it raises awareness. Diana earned the title of "people's princess" not just because of her bond with the British people, but also because of the adoring crowds around the world. She earned it by caring for people in need, including the forgotten, the oppressed, the sick, and the hungry.

Millions of tears were shed in the aftermath of Diana's untimely death, as the love she gave the world would no longer be felt. Diana's unselfish, humanitarian efforts cannot be judged entirely on their own, but they will go on as her legacy.

CHAPTER 1:
The Princess's Birth

Among the millions of baby boomer girls frolicking around England's cities and countryside in the mid-1960s, few would have been deemed more likely to marry into the royal family than Diana Spencer. But no one in the British nobility could have predicted this lonely, contemplative kid becoming a princess and growing into one of history's most cherished and admired ladies.

It seems only natural that a newborn who will bring so much joy to others would arrive in the early summer. Diana Frances Spencer was born in her Norfolk, England, home in the late afternoon on July 1, 1961. She was the youngest of three daughters born to Edward John Spencer (nicknamed "Johnnie") and his first wife Frances. Though the 7-pound, 12-ounce baby was physically perfect, Johnnie was disappointed that yet another birth had failed to produce a male heir to carry on the Spencer name.

In fact, the couple was so certain Frances would give birth to a male that they hadn't even considered what to name a girl. They didn't choose Diana Frances until a week after the baby was born, combining the names of the infant's mother and an eighteenth-century Spencer ancestress who died when she was a toddler. Johnnie's angst over the lack of a male child had reached a boiling point. When Frances gave birth to a boy, William and Frances had already begun raising their daughters Elizabeth Sarah and Cynthia Jane. However, infant John was so severely malformed and unwell that he only lived for 10 hours. Frances' baby was taken away from her shortly after birth, with little explanation. It was the last time she saw her son. For years, Frances lamented the fact that she had never held John. His life had been cut short due to a lung problem. However, Frances' depression over her baby's death did not prevent her from immediately attempting to conceive again. As a result, Diana was born, adding to the family's sadness at not having a male heir. Despite his desire for a son, Johnnie had a special affinity for Diana.

Diana recognized troubles in the family from an early age, stemming from the lack of a male child to carry on the Spencer name. Her mother was taken to several London clinics to investigate the phenomenon. Frances, who was only 25 years old when she gave birth to Diana, was humiliated and enraged by what she saw as unfair and needless examinations. Frances' marital discontent grew as a result of that incident, the roots of which were planted when her infant baby died. Diana was never given the opportunity to be raised by parents who had a happy marriage. Diana soon developed feelings of remorse and failure as a result of not being born a boy. As physically rich as her childhood was, it was also emotionally deficient. Such bad ideas and beliefs harmed her early mind and did not go away till she was a young adult. When Frances later gave birth to a son, Charles Edward, his entrance was met with even more pomp and circumstance. Diana was baptized in a Sandringham church, and her godparents were affluent commoners. The ceremony for her brother took place at the famed Westminster Abbey, with Queen Elizabeth serving as the main godparent.

The Better Side

Diana treasured the joys of her youth despite such clear contrasts in treatment and respect. Years after she had achieved recognition as Princess of Wales, she revealed her delight in the most basic sensory sensations. She recalled the scent of plastic inside her first stroller, a powerful recollection given how young she was at the time. However, those joyous and carefree moments were rare and far between. Diana spent her early life wondering and frequently believing she was nothing more than a brother to her family, especially her parents. She was convinced that if the infant John had survived, she would not have been born. It is impossible to say if such feelings were legitimate or imposed. Family members frequently recalled Diana's rejection as a result of her shock at John's death. Diana's second cousin, Robert Spencer, thought Diana had low self-esteem as a child.

Diana was surrounded by a lively and joyful atmosphere at Park House, which was located near a woodland region approximately six miles from the Norfolk shore. She was amazed by its size, which contained opulent amenities like tennis courts, an outdoor swimming pool, and a cricket pitch. The staff of six, which included a butler, a cook, and a private governess, lived in their own private cottages. Swimming was one of Diana's favorite activities. Children benefit emotionally from demonstrating talent, and she was no exception. Adult acceptance boosted her self-esteem, particularly in her swimming. Despite her father's disapproval of her diving off the board at such a young age, she would call to anyone within hearing distance so that all eyes were on her as she made a precise dive into the pool.

Diana, like most children, was ignorant to much of her surroundings, particularly items that didn't interest her. She spent a lot of time in a classroom where governess Gertrude Allen taught her and her sisters how to read and write. Diana also appreciated the company of a ginger-colored cat named Marmalade, as well as the atmosphere in "The Beatle Room," which the kids decorated with posters and other memorabilia honoring the Fab Four, their favorite rock and roll group. Diana's first-floor bedroom was just as appealing. She might look out her window at the grazing cattle or the frolicking rabbits and foxes on the grass. Her affection for animals appeared limitless. Throughout her childhood, she cared for hamsters, rabbits, guinea pigs, and a goldfish, whom she referred to as family members. When a pet died, she gently placed it in a shoebox, which she buried in a hole on the grass beneath a spreading cedar tree. She even made her own small crosses to place on their graves. Her fondness for all things furry or feathery would become a defining feature of her upbringing. Her sympathy for the defenseless persisted throughout her life. She took excellent care of the animals she cherished as a child, and she kept the animals and their habitats absolutely clean. She realized how much they relied on her.

Diana and her siblings spent their more active and carefree hours feeding lake trout at adjacent Sandringham House, a place originally constructed to accommodate guests when Park House was full. She liked going on walks with her spaniel and swimming in the pool. She was three years old when she first discovered the delights and difficulties of horseback riding. Few British children could have been spoiled more than Diana, albeit nanny Judith Parnell did a lot of the pampering. Diana knew Parnell much better than she knew her own parents. Diana was nine years old the first time she and her father shared a meal at the downstairs dining room table. Her parents were nice to her, but she didn't feel close to them. It was a romance from another period, one of affluence but devoid of emotion. Diana was worried despite her luxurious surroundings and seemingly unlimited amount of mindless pursuits. Her self-esteem plummeted more as her parents' marital difficulties worsened. Various tabloid reports have strongly implied, if not outright stated, that Johnnie frequently tormented and even physically struck his wife, which may have contributed to Diana's difficult and guilt-ridden childhood. The Spencers have always disputed the allegations. Friends and family have also expressed their disbelief that violence was ever a factor, though they concede Johnnie was afflicted by a temper that had become a family trait. He had inherited Spencer's notorious temper—but violence? According to individuals close to Johnnie, this is not the case. Family relatives believe that, despite his insensitive nature, Johnnie never displayed any of these characteristics. Many believe he desired to be ruled by Frances.

With time, the age and personality disparities between Johnnie and Frances, who was 12 years younger than her husband, become more pronounced and destructive. Diana's father preferred to stay at home, whilst her mother sought to expand her wings and explore the social opportunities available to members of the British aristocracy. She frequently traveled to London for parties. Frances just became bored being in Norfolk, owing in part to her youth. Her resentment of her husband's behavior, as well as a gnawing, developing feeling that there was more to life than being a wife and mother, drove her to seek fulfillment outside the home. Frances, after all, got engaged at the age of 17 and married a year later.

Johnnie became enraged by her unhappiness and wild side. Frances met a young guy named Peter Shand Kydd at a dinner party in London during the summer of 1966, around the time Diana was celebrating her fifth birthday. Shand Kydd's family had made a fortune in the wallpaper industry, but he had preferred to operate his sheep ranch in Australia. He returned to London after that failed. They have a lot in common. Shand Kydd was married with three children. They soon became more than just pals. Shand Kydd and Frances were having an affair by the time he divorced his wife of 16 years in early 1967. Her attraction to Shand Kydd, along with her dwindling feelings for her husband, caused her to fall in love with her new beau. Frances and Johnnie's marriage was on borrowed time. The couple decided on a trial separation in the summer of 1967. Separations and divorces were significantly less common in the 1960s than they are now, so the announcement surprised friends and family. It was extremely upsetting to the four youngsters.

Many of those who blamed Frances for the breakup accused her of abandoning her children to be with Shand Kydd, but she had actually planned for Charles and Diana to join her in her rented apartment in Belgravia, a central London district. Diana attended the Francis

Holland School, while Charles attended the adjoining kindergarten. Sarah and Jane were at boarding school at the time. Fran-ces hoped that the children would be unharmed by what was supposed to be a brief separation. On weekends, Charles and Diana would visit their father, and the entire family would sometimes be present when Johnnie paid them a visit in Belgravia. The family occasionally returned to Park House for short visits, notably over the holidays. When the entire family stayed together, the atmosphere was downright depressing. It was clear that Johnnie and France's relationship would never be the same. Even young Diana and Charles sensed that the trial separation would be permanent. They cried a lot about it, but Frances saw the separation as preferable to the tension and hostility that had seized the house when she and Johnnie were together.

Marriage's Death Knell

During the 1967 holiday season, the final chapter of the breakup was written. After Frances requested a divorce, an enraged and resentful Johnnie enrolled Diana and Charles at new schools near his home without informing his wife. Why, he wondered, should Frances have the children after she abandoned him? Frances couldn't oppose the move because the courts were closed for the holidays. She had no choice but to return to London without her two children. She tried unsuccessfully to bring her children back after the New Year. She wasn't even permitted to enter Park House. Frances recalls once banging on the door and pleading with the butler to let her in, but she was refused. Frances was heartbroken because she wanted to reassure her children that she had not abandoned them, but they couldn't hear her outside their home. Diana, who was six years old at the time, recalled her mother's angry departure, which shattered all prospect of reunion. Her sentiments were not soothed as the divorce proceedings became more harsh in the winter and spring of 1968. The kids were thrown into the center of a custody fight. Frances had precedent on her side: the mother was usually awarded custody of the children. She sought custody of the children, but her affair with Shand Kydd worked against her. Ruth, her mother, even testified against her.

It was unsurprising that the court granted Johnnie custody of the children based on Frances' adultery. But, because Frances and Shand Kydd married on May 2, 1969, and acquired a property on West Sussex's Atlantic coast, it may not have mattered who got custody. Diana would suffer greatly as a result of her parents' separation and subsequent divorce. Diana, after all, had never had a completely healthy family life. She was just five years old when her parents divorced. She had never had constant, loving touch with either of her parents before that. She still felt guilty about being born a girl. And she was far too little to comprehend the emotional anguish she was experiencing. "My parents were too busy sorting themselves out," Diana explained. "I remember my mother crying, and daddy never told us anything about it." We were never allowed to ask questions. There are far too many nannies. The entire situation was highly unstable."

Diana put up a strong front despite the fact that she couldn't totally hide her dissatisfaction. She was always playing with her various toys, racing around the driveway on her blue tricycle and riding her many dolls in her stroller. Her inherent urge to care for others, which defined her maturity, was already a strong feature of her character. However, her anxieties were exacerbated both before and after the divorce by a lack of parental affection and emotional support. She and Charles were both terrified of the dark. The fluffy critters that were so entertaining during the day turned terrifying at night when they went about their business outside Park House. And Johnnie didn't help matters. He once told Diana and Charles that a murderer was on the loose in the region. They stayed awake with their eyes wide open, terrified and closely listening for any sound that may suggest the murderer had broken into their home. Charles grieved uncontrollably for his mother when she left. Diana wished she could be a mother figure to him during those sleepless evenings, but her fear of the dark kept her from leaving her bed to console him. She was filled with melancholy as well, but she couldn't summon the fortitude to emerge from under her blanket and care for her brother.

The employment of nannies to care for Diana and Charles had become a revolving door by that point. Some were nice, but others were rude and unforgiving. One nanny had to be fired because she had chastised Sarah and Jane by putting laxatives in their food. When Diana and Charles misbehaved, another sadistically hit them on the head with a wooden spoon. Though other nannies were nice, they couldn't compare to Frances in the hearts and minds of the children, who saw them all as inadequate substitutes for her. The kids got together to make their nannies' lives miserable, performing tricks such as locking them in the toilet and throwing their clothes out the window.

Johnnie's plight didn't make things any easier. Despite his children's kindness and thoughtfulness, he submerged himself in his work to avoid drowning in bad thoughts. He was still upset at Frances for being unfaithful and causing the divorce, but he never reprimanded her in front of the children. Carefree and joyous moments, like when he brought in a camel for Diana's surprise birthday celebration on her seventh birthday, were rare during those bleak early 1970s. Johnnie was simply overburdened with work and parenting.

School provided little relief for the children. They felt alone because they were the only students in the building with divorced parents. The teachers attempted to assist, despite the fact that they were warm and friendly with all of their students. Because the school had only 40 students, each child received a significant level of individual attention. Toward the end of Diana's time there, one teacher came to an unsettling conclusion about Diana's mindset. She wrote about Diana's defeatist attitude and a bleak future if that weakness was not overcome. Diana was reserved with her classmates, both inside and outside of the classroom. Her jumbled thinking during that time in her life also had an impact on her studies. She was often so upset that she burst into tears in class, which shocked both the teacher and the pupils. Unfortunately, her artwork was always dedicated to her estranged parents.

Diana felt jealousy toward Charles, who had received acclaim from his teachers for his studious demeanor, behavior, and success in the classroom, at this point. She craved favorable attention. It wasn't always enough for her to be proud of her accomplishments, such as swimming and dancing. She felt the urge for others to notice and appreciate her. Despite the difficulty in her relationship with Charles, she felt closer to him than to her two elder sisters, owing to the fact that they spent the most of their time away at boarding school. Diana was protective of her younger brother since she had strong maternal instincts even as a small child. After the divorce, his sorrow became her suffering. Diana was also prone to stretching the truth. Her parents' divorce exacerbated the situation. In one case, a school official driving Diana home threatened to kick her out of the car if she told one more lie.

The house she was referring to was Park House, although Diana and Charles didn't have just one. They spent every weekend and two weeks over the Christmas holidays with their mother in London. Frances cried many tears during those times because of the court's decision to limit the amount of time she could spend with them. Even when Diana and Charles were in her presence, she missed them. Frances sobbed as she contemplated her children's departure at the conclusion of the weekend. Her children felt the same way about hopping from one house to the other during the holidays. They received several gifts, but not nearly enough time to be loved and appreciated by either parent.

Away from Home

Diana took a much-needed break from Park House in 1970, when she enrolled at Riddlesworth Hall, a two-hour drive away in Norfolk. Her father's rejection prompted her to resist at first, but she quickly warmed up to the idea. Diana had an academic and social outlet thanks to Riddlesworth. She was not only taught English, arithmetic, history, and science, but she also had personal experience in living and interacting with others. Riddlesworth, like many boarding schools, stressed social skills such as correct etiquette. Diana was given the opportunity to care for her favorite animals as well as those of her classmates as the head of the Pets' Corner at Riddlesworth. Peanuts, one of the pets, earned first place for "Best Kept Guinea Pig."

Despite her physical growth—she continued to excel in swimming and diving—Diana was an average student in school. She just fit in with the other students, but when John-nie dropped off and picked up his daughter, the staff took note. His lively and kind nature stood out. Patricia Wood, the headmaster, and her staff agree that they recall Johnnie far more vividly than Diana, who simply blended in with the other girls at Riddlesworth.

Diana would inherit her father's genuine concern and interest in people. Though it would be many years before she was confident enough in herself to bloom socially, such characteristics would eventually make her one of the twentieth century's most adored individuals. How did Diana's illustrious family background influence her upbringing and adult life? An examination of her ancestors explains a lot.

CHAPTER 2:
A Family Tree

During the more difficult times in her life, Diana would often tell herself, "Remember you're Spencer."1 She pronounced those words with a strong sense of pride. They advised her to toughen up at difficult emotional periods. After all, the Spencers had a long history of wealth, success, and reputation in Britain.

The family's prosperity could be traced back to the Glorious Revolution of 1688, when the Whigs helped topple King Charles II and gave the kingdom to George I, putting the Whig thinkers in power until the early nineteenth century. Though party politics did not emerge in Britain until after the American Revolution, the Whigs had established themselves as a group battling against absolute government and allied with Britain's great aristocratic families. The Whig populist ideas were shared by the Spencers of those eras. They had already amassed enormous money from sheep husbandry and wool selling. The family possessed vast expanses of land in Warwickshire, Northamptonshire, Buckinghamshire, and Hertfordshire by the 1400s. In 1508 John Spencer erected a family center residence at Althorp. The 121-room palace was set on 13,000 acres. The Whigs were described as the "most serious, exclusive, and illustrious cousinhood, held together by birth, blood, and breeding," by historian David Cannadine. "They were the embodiment of glamor and grandeur, high rank and high living."

The Spencers expanded into what is now Greater London over the next two centuries. They had property in Claphan, Wandsworth, and Wimbledon. Despite their kinship to the royal dynasties of Charles II and James II, the aristocratic Spencers regarded themselves to be of higher social standing. The Spencers did not keep their fortune to themselves. They bought high-society artifacts like rare books and artwork and displayed them throughout Althorp House. The expensive collection was very important to Johnnie's father, Jack, the 7th Earl Spencer. However, Jack's son felt claustrophobic staying inside, guarding the jewels. He enjoyed outdoor activities from a young age. Such disparities in personalities and priorities affected Jack and Johnnie's relationship. Jack's notorious temper did not help to calm things down.

The theory that opposites attract was certainly bolstered by Jack and his wife, Cynthia, the daughter of the Duke of Aber-corn. While Jack exemplified aristocratic arrogance, Cynthia was sensitive and compassionate to people from all walks of life. Diana gradually inherited skills like empathy and concern towards others. The Spencer family never reached nor sought power, but their wealth and illustrious ancestors made them well-known in the political sphere. The Spencers have held positions as Knights of the Garter, First Lord of the Admiralty, and ambassadors throughout history. Seven American presidents and actor Humphrey Bogart were among their relatives.

Frances' forefathers were no less powerful. The Fermoys made their impact in Ireland early on. Edmund Burke Roche, Diana's great-great-grandfather, was elected to the Irish Parliament and eventually became a baron. James Roche married Frances (Fanny) Work, whose father, Frank, was a wealthy stockbroker who brought huge quantities of money into the family. However, the marriage failed, and Frank threatened to withhold the flow of such wealth into the family unless grandsons Maurice and Francis were educated in America. The grandchildren fulfilled their grandfather's goal, prompting Frank to leave Maurice and Francis $2.9 million each when he died in 1911. In 1921, the two men returned to England with their money. Maurice fell in love with Ruth Gill, a beautiful Scottish pianist half his age who would become Diana's grandmother. Maurice had developed a close relationship with

British royalty. He became acquainted with the Duke of York, who later became King George VI, and Ruth and Queen Elizabeth formed a close bond because they both loved music. The Fermoys were in charge of purchasing Park House in Norfolk. The lease was given to Diana's grandfather, Maurice, also known as the 4th Baron Fermoy, who finally landed in the British Parliament.

A New Generation

Frances was the second of three children born to Maurice and Ruth in 1936. She was nurtured in an elite household, surrounded by nannies and governesses. She learnt perfect decorum in all aspects of her personal and social life, and she adored and respected her parents. Her father was caring and empathetic, and she praised her mother's confidence and ambition. The Roche siblings were in turmoil, whether or not it was related to their parents' upbringing. After Ruth died, Frances's sister Mary went through three divorces and lived in seclusion in London. Edmund, the 5th Baron Fermoy, suffered from depression and committed suicide at the age of 45 in 1984. During her youth, Frances demonstrated considerable intelligence and a love of the arts, but she was far from snobbish or dull. Rather, she had a great sense of humor. She had a commanding personality, which drew Johnnie to her.

That romance began in April 1953, six months after her 17th birthday, at a coming-out ball in London. Johnnie was not only 12 years older than Frances, but he was also engaged to Lady Anne Coke, the eldest daughter of the Earl and Countess of Leicester and the same age as Frances. Frances's attractiveness took Johnnie aback. He promptly called off his engagement and began dating Frances. When Johnnie asked for her hand in marriage during a break from playing tennis at Park House, the couple were engaged. Frances ignored the age discrepancy, knowing that Fer-moy women had a long history of marrying considerably older men. Despite a previous commitment that had taken Johnnie to Australia for six months, the agreement remained firm. In June 1954, the couple married at Westminster Abbey. Among those representing the royal family at the meeting of over 1,000 guests were Queen Elizabeth and Prince Philip.

After honeymooning throughout Europe, Johnnie and Frances lived in a house on the grounds of Althorp, but their polar opposite feelings for those hallowed halls exacerbated their clash of personalities. Frances thought her house was drab. She thought their collection of beautiful artwork and porcelain made their home feel more like a museum than a homey home. Though Frances declared her happiness early in their marriage and quickly set out to have children ("honeymoon baby" Sarah was born nine months after the wedding), she was turned off by Jack and Johnnie's incessant fighting. She also began to feel restless, which would eventually contribute to the marriage's dissolution. Her independence rankled the Spencers, who were staunchly conservative. Johnnie, on the other hand, was open to his new wife's wishes. After Maurice's death in 1955, she and Johnnie moved into Park House. Frances inherited around $300,000, allowing the couple to acquire an additional 236 acres of land, doubling their previous area. Johnnie farmed the property and became more involved with charity, especially the National Association of Boys' Clubs.

The first few years at Park House were idyllic. The couple traveled frequently and maintained contacts with their aristocratic acquaintances. Frances relished the prospect of beginning a family, but the death of baby John changed everything. It threw a cloud over the marriage that never lifted. Diana was far too young to understand the reasons for her parents' divorce during the early stages, yet she intuitively sensed there was a problem. She was already demonstrating ancestor-inherited personality traits as a toddler. She, like grandmother Cynthia, sincerely cared about those who were less fortunate. She, like Johnnie, has a natural capacity to communicate with others. And, like Frances, her strong determination was evident from a young age.

She, like Frances, despised her visits to the Althorp mansion, which just terrified her. She didn't understand its history, as one could expect from a little youngster. Other youngsters might have found the eerie corridors and images of deceased ancestors appealing, but not Diana—or her brother. Charles remembered Althorp as impersonal and overbearing, like a bygone era's club where the ticking of clocks irritated its visitors. He thought it was especially uninviting and even frightening for youngsters. It's no surprise he objected when told he was going there as a child. They had no option when Johnnie relocated the family to Althorp after Jack died abruptly of pneumonia in 1975.

Diana was now an adolescent, and her skills and flaws were more apparent. Despite the fact that her sister Jane was by far the strongest student in the family, Diana adored the rebellious Sarah, for whom she did endless errands. But Diana was never one to complain about doing her own tasks or helping others. She was awarded the Legett Cup for her helpfulness at Riddlesworth, which thrilled Diana's grandmother, Countess Cynthia Spencer, who shared Diana's sense of kinship. Cynthia's death from a brain tumor in 1972 came as a surprise to the sensitive child. Diana, who was sad, believed that her grandma still spiritually protected her.

Following in the Steps of Her Sisters

Diana quickly followed Sarah and Jane to the Kent boarding school West Heath. West Heath, like Riddlesworth, strove to instill confidence and character in its students; its emphasis was only partially academic. But which sister would Diana choose to follow? Will she follow in the footsteps of her elder sister Sarah, who, despite her participation in theater and swimming, was expelled for lack of discipline at one point? Or would she follow in the footsteps of Jane, a well-mannered and talented student who took the straight and narrow path? Charles, too, had excelled academically at Maidwell Hall in Northamptonshire, a forerunner to his collegiate stint at Oxford.

Diana appeared to prefer the former early in her West Heath tenure. She relished the opportunity to escape the monotony of life in West Heath. She took one dare to travel a half mile down the driveway in the middle of the night to get some candy from Polly Phillimore. She completed her duty only to realize that no one was present. She returned down the long driveway as police cars arrived and found that all of the lights in the school had been switched on. She later realized that the police presence was caused by one of her roommates complaining of appendicitis, not by her absence. Diana's boarding school enrollment was nearly jeopardized as a result of the act, but she reasoned that life was very boring, so why not try a dare? Diana's divorced parents were summoned to the school, although neither was upset with her. In fact, her father was overjoyed that his hitherto timid daughter had exhibited such bravery. Diana continued to take risks, such as consuming massive amounts of food in one sitting, despite the fact that it occasionally placed her in the company of the school nurse. Diana was skeptical of adults and generally moderately unfriendly to her peers, according to West Heath principal Ruth Rudge, who claimed not to remember the incident. Diana bloomed, according to Rudge, when she got to know and understand the people she hung out with. She thought adults had to earn her trust before she would open up to them.

Carolyn Pride (later Carolyn Bartholomew), a longtime friend who shared Diana's dormitory room and later shared her London flat, recalled a striking difference between Diana's and Jane's behavior. Diana and Carolyn had the unpleasant distinction of being two of the few students at West Heath who had divorced parents. Carolyn thought Diana was significantly more vivacious than Jane, who she thought was popular and kind but somewhat bland. Diana struggled in school at West Heath. Despite her preference for courses involving people, such as history, and her enjoyment of writing, she did poorly on tests. Grades of "D," which meant failing at West Heath, were widespread.

While Diana struggled to match her siblings' academic accomplishments, another side of her continued to emerge. She began to put her passion to help people into action. As a child, she felt pity for her animals; now, she feels sympathy for elders, as well as the physically and mentally ill. Darenth Park, a hospital for the physically and mentally handicapped, was one of the places Diana visited at the time. It was an intimidating location for the West Heath students, who had little experience engaging with these people. Muriel Stevens, the trip's organizer, was impressed with Diana's handling of the matter. The majority of the disabled persons were in wheelchairs, and some were encouraged to leave their seats to greet the visitors. Many patients approached them or grabbed them, frightening many of the students. Diana, on the other hand, just felt more sympathy for the sick. Stevens described her as relaxed and in her element, which she thought was wonderful.

Diana and a classmate made weekly visits to a senior in Sevenoaks. They shared tea, biscuits, and conversation with her before assisting her with her shopping. During the same time period, she went to a nearby mental hospital and delighted the patients by dancing with them. She not only conducted volunteer work, but she learned that she actually cared about those who were less fortunate and that she was gifted in this area. Those she worked with admired and valued her personality. Diana seemed to sincerely care about them. Such accomplishments boosted her self-esteem, as they do for many young people.

Her physical and artistic abilities flourished. Diana not only excelled as a swimmer and diver, winning multiple competitions, but she was also an excellent tennis player. In 1976, she won her school dancing competition while studying piano. Diana adored athletics and the arts, but she preferred to thrive in areas where her sisters and predecessors had not yet established themselves. Grandmother Cynthia and her sister Sarah were also accomplished pianists. Her mother and sisters were successful athletes. Diana disliked her family's engagement in her interest in sports and the arts. This could not be said of her community service, which boosted her self-esteem because no one else was involved in her accomplishments. After the family relocated to Althorp, she practiced her ballet exclusively when no family or friends were there. Diana enjoyed a variety of sports and dance styles, but tap dancing was one of her favorites. She rejected claims that she ignored some scholastic subjects. Though she did not thrive in some of them, she later spoke about her love of the piano, tap dance, and sports including tennis, netball, and hockey.

"Raine, Raine, Go Away"

Diana soon gained another significant adult in her life: Countess of Dartmouth Raine Legge, with whom Johnnie established a romantic relationship. When the family was still living at Park House in 1972, the couple met. The lovely countess, who had a strong brain and a motivated personality, was married with four children when she fell in love with Johnnie. The four Spencer children colluded to ruin her first date with their father. They believed Johnnie to be theirs alone, and anyone who attempted to infiltrate his personal life was viewed as an intruder. Lady Dartmouth did not recognise the girls' frigid treatment of her when she arrived at Park House for lunch. She, on the other hand, remained cordial. Sarah is determined to escalate her impoliteness. Her father chastised her for belching so loudly and purposefully. Sarah responded sarcastically that belching is a gesture of appreciation in Arab cultures, to which her father asked her to leave the table.

Diana swiftly took Sarah's side. When Johnnie reprimanded her to stay quiet, she claimed she wasn't feeling well and asked to be excused. Her embarrassed father swiftly dismissed her as well.

The children's disdain of Raine, especially given that it was their first meeting, may be defined as sheer envy. But Charles remembered their objections against her going beyond that, even if they couldn't be pinpointed. He and his siblings had an inherent dislike and suspicion towards her. Lady Dartmouth was not at all deterred. She was well recognized as the daughter of Barbara Cartland, Diana's favorite novelist. She was a driven lady both emotionally and professionally. On several councils, she had established a reputation as a strong-willed lady. As chairperson of the Historic Buildings Board and a member of the English Tourist Board, she advanced her career. Lady Dartmouth was also involved in politics. Some praised her for resigning from a government advisory committee on the environment, while others chastised her. Her name became even more well-known throughout the country as a result of her gorgeous features, fashionable attire, and ability to rise to positions of authority. Raine and Johnnie's friendship was fostered by their business relationship, as Johnnie appreciated women with strong personalities. She wrote a book titled What Is Our Heritage? while chairperson of the United Kingdom Executive Committee for European Architectural Heritage in 1975, which was committed to protecting ancient towns and buildings. She requested Johnnie to assist the cause by serving as head of the National Association of Boys' Clubs.

The attraction between Johnnie and Raine was palpable. Raine posed a challenge to Diana, who adored taking care of her father and considered herself the apple of his eye. Raine's increased presence in

Diana's life, along with the transfer to Althorp, both grieved and enraged her. She not only lost her pals from Norfolk, but she also received an uncomfortable prospective stepmother. Raine had showered her and her brothers with presents, but she was afraid Raine would take their father away from them.

Diana also mourned the warmth of Park House and its surroundings. Despite being nestled in the magnificent rolling hills of the English countryside, the Althorp mansion exuded a haughty, frigid, imperious air. Diana, on the other hand, grew to enjoy Althorp's illustrious history and kept herself occupied with home chores and even preparing her specialty, bread and butter pudding, for the servants. She and her siblings had overcome their childhood terror of Althorp and began to appreciate its treasures, such as the front staircase, which they slid down on a tea tray.

Raine moved in shortly after, and all joy for the children vanished. She hadn't yet married Johnnie, but she was invited to stay in a room near her future husband's. The kids didn't mind that their mother had a lot of money, some of which she spent on redecorating Althorp. She began to worry that her hatred toward the Spencer children would jeopardize her aspirations to marry Johnnie. Sarah, as the eldest and possibly the most opposed to Raine, took the initiative in seeking to persuade her. In an attempt to poison the relationship, she even utilized the media to disparage her father's girlfriend. Diana and her siblings would sometimes chant, "Raine, Raine, go away" within hearing distance of Lady Dartmouth. But she wasn't going anywhere, not with Johnnie in her sights. Gerald Dartmouth was awarded a divorce for adultery in May 1976, allowing her to marry Johnnie two months later in London. He didn't want to enrage his children before the wedding, so he waited until afterward to tell them. The delay just fueled their rage. Sarah, who discovered the news from a newspaper story rather than her father, informed Diana that they had a new, unwanted stepmother. Diana challenged Johnnie, which resulted in a fairly violent confrontation:

> [**Johnnie**] said, "I want to explain to you why, um, I've got mar-ried to Raine." And I said, "Well, we don't like her." And he said, "I know that, but you'll grow to love her, as I have." And I said, "Well, we won't." I kept on saying we, not I. I was the little crusader here . . . and I got really angry and I, if I remem-ber rightly, I slapped him across the face, and I said, "That's from all of us, for hurting us" and walked out of the room and slammed the door. He followed me and he got me by the wrist and turned me around and said, "Don't you ever talk to me like that again." And I said, "Well, don't you ever do that to us again," and walked off.

Though Diana never warmed to Althorp, she disliked Raine for selling various pieces of the huge collection housed in the magnificent estate in order to pay inheritance taxes and fund the changes she wished. Diana believed that the bright, glittering aesthetic produced by the new Countess Spencer had erased the historical majesty and whatever homey atmosphere Althorp had when they moved in.

While Diana was bitter and upset over the permanent addition of Raine to the family, Sarah was deeply impacted. She had fallen in love with the Duke of Westminster, Gerald Grosvenor. The romance was meant to end in marriage, according to relatives and friends, but it did so fairly quickly. The emotionally distraught young woman quickly developed an eating disorder, which was blamed on the breakup. The once-beautiful and vibrant oldest Spencer sibling withered away, weighing only 77 pounds. Sarah suffered from both anorexia and bulimia. She starved herself at times, but she also ate excessively before self-induced vomiting. Such diseases were not widely recognized until at least a decade later, but Sarah remembered feeling gaunt. She was obliged to shop in the children's section, but she refused to recognize she had a problem. Even though she was frail, she convinced herself that she was lovely. Diana was very worried. Her sister tried to conceal Sarah's eating condition when she visited her at her apartment when she was away from West Heath. Diana, on the other hand, couldn't help but notice her already-slim sister's 35-pound weight loss

CHAPTER 3:
Diana, the Adolescent

Diana had no idea that she would later become a victim of the same eating disorders as Sarah had, despite signs of obsessive behavior, particularly with regard to food. After all, the young girl happily accepted school dares to eat three kippers and six pieces of bread. It's unclear whether she was purging at the time.

Anorexia had been recognised by the psychiatric establishment by that point, but bulimia was a different story. The research of various eating disorders would not become more prevalent until the following decades. Diana's voracious eating habits were frequently mentioned by those close to her at West Heath. Even she admitted to having a huge appetite. She would gorge herself on midnight snacks, breaking the rules by taking food into her room. Despite this, the amount of food she ate did not cause her to gain weight.

Diana's obsessive conduct had been a part of her life for years. Even at the age of six, when most children's bedrooms look like they've been hit by a storm, Diana maintained hers immaculate. During her elementary school years, she even tidied up after her friends. It has been suggested that Diana's compulsive need to manage her weight and surroundings sprang from her overpowering feelings of stress as a youngster. Dr. Kent Ravenscroft, a child and adolescent psychiatrist and psychoanalyst, suggested that Diana's neatness was an extension of her attempt to clean up her terrible feelings.1 He claimed that her inclinations to be messy were conquered by a drive to put things in order and regulate her life.

Binging and purging were also options. Diana's personal eating disorders as a teen were not widely reported until she openly discussed them shortly before her death in 1997. Previously, she blamed the illness on the frigid treatment she received from Prince Charles during their engagement. She then acknowledged that she had developed bulimia a few years before. She told patients at Roehampton Priory, a private treatment south of London, that she blamed her eating disorder on her idolization of Sarah.

The girl who would later develop into a gorgeous princess and the world's most photographed lady did not attract attention. She also did not exude the grace and charm of royalty to strangers. Diana, who had always been attractive, appeared gangly and awkward as a young adolescent. Such insecurity is normal at that age, but individuals from aristocratic households are treated differently. Lucinda Craig Harvey, Sarah's London housemate who met Diana during a cricket match at Althorp, was among many who had a terrible first impression of Diana. Harvey criticized Diana's unattractive clothing, as well as her overall timidity and unsophisticated demeanor.

Diana's mental state during that time period was influenced by her father's marriage to Raine. She was quite sensitive, and she saw herself as stupid, especially in comparison to her siblings. During her final years at West Heath, her jealousy of Charles grew stronger. Her failure to pass two crucial sets of tests that would have resulted in her promotion prompted her to drop out at the age of 16. Diana's lack of academic success has been linked to a number of causes. She still had the impression that her parents had given birth to her solely to replace baby John, who died on his first day. She felt guilty for not being born a male. It is evident that she felt betrayed by her father, whom she regarded as lost to Raine. Classmates and classmates, on the other hand, have stated that Diana's poor academic performance was simply the product of her lethargy at the time.

Diana's Feeling of Destiny

Some people believed Diana was guided by a deep sense of her ultimate place in the world. Diana, according to biographer Sarah Bradford, developed an inner conviction in herself and her instincts that led her throughout her life. She went on to say that Diana believed she had a higher calling that set her apart from others.2 If that was the case, academics might not have appeared so significant, but Diana was upset by her academic failure. It seemed to solidify the image of her that she imagined her family had. She expressed hopelessness and despair, which she turned into jealousy of Charles, who excelled intellectually. Her assumption that her family thought she was stupid wounded her. Diana recalls crying in the headmistress's company about her failings.

Raine was getting all of Johnnie's attention at a time when Diana needed comfort from her father. Rather than cultivating a strong inclusive relationship with all family members, she competed with the children for Johnnie's attention. And he didn't mind because he was attracted to dominant ladies. He always loved and showed love to his children, but many family members believe he let Raine use the situation to her advantage. Raine, a social butterfly with a slew of wealthy and prominent friends, frequently threw parties at Althorp during which the kids were sent away. Raine didn't always need to act on her possessiveness because the kids were away at boarding school for the majority of the time. She had Johnnie completely to herself.

Diana's dissatisfaction was directed inward despite her academic difficulties. To those close to her, she rarely showed rage or bitterness. Her popularity soared among the Althorp personnel. Butler Ainslie Pendrey and his housekeeper wife, Maud, who were drawn to Diana's shyness during the girl's visits every six or seven weeks, were one couple that loved her company. When Diana came home, Ainslie would make sure all of her favorite dishes were on hand in the kitchen. They admired her courtesy and didn't mind indulging her. Diana ultimately revealed herself to the pair, which they appreciated. They also discussed how the entire staff appreciated her pleasant personality and how Diana would always find an arrangement of flowers on her bed when she arrived at Althorp. Diana, according to Ainsley, will be something spectacular someday.

Diana needed to get away from her academic life for a while before she could truly develop. She accompanied Sarah to the Institut Alpin Videmanette, a finishing school in Switzerland for the affluent that enrolled largely Spanish and Italian girls but imposed a requirement that students speak French. Diana not only continued to speak English, but she became dissatisfied with her classwork in the stereotypically female home science course. Furthermore, she simply did not want to go to school any longer. Skiing was all she wanted to do in Switzerland. She wrote her parents letter after letter, sometimes four a day, begging them to let her come home. She said that they were squandering their money and her time by keeping her at a school hundreds of miles away from her home, which she despised. She eventually persuaded them to let her go home.

Another chapter in Diana's relationship with her father and stepmother was written in September 1978, one that solidified her sentiments for both. During a visit with friends in Norfolk, she had a strong feeling that Johnnie would become ill and even die. The following day, while strolling through the Althorp courtyard, Johnnie fainted from a major cerebral hemorrhage. He was transported to Northampton General Hospital unconscious. Raine was not satisfied with the facilities and insisted on transporting her husband to the National Hospital for Nervous Diseases in London. Johnnie had lapsed into a coma and was placed on life support at the age of 54. Raine stayed by his side, hoping desperately for his survival. For four hours, surgeons worked tirelessly on his brain. Johnnie appeared to be recovering, but he was transferred to Brompton Hospital less than a month later after contracting a rare infection that was untreatable by standard antibiotics.

Raine refuses to give up hope despite multiple near-death experiences. In what looked to be a futile quest to find a new treatment that could save her husband's life, she called acquaintance Bill Cavendish-Bentnick, the director of German pharmaceutical giant Bayer, who eventually became Duke of Portland. There was one, after all—a test product named Azlocillin. The use of a new medicine would necessitate consent from Johnnie's doctors, who eventually agreed. It worked fantastically well. Raine had literally saved his life.

Raine's devotion to their father did not result in a healthier and warmer relationship between Raine and the children. Instead, they only went to see their father when Raine was not there. When they finally met, the children were nothing but mockery. Diana believed Raine was preventing her and her siblings from visiting their father, prompting Sarah to take the lead in attempting to get them into the hospital, which was largely futile. They worried that their father simply assumed his children didn't want to see him. The episode heightened tensions between Raine and the children even further. But, as usual, their stepmother was unflappable. She used the "me against them" strategy once more. While Diana and her siblings were protesting that nurses had been instructed to keep them away from their critically ill father, Raine stated that it was the children who tried to keep her away. "I'm a survivor, and people who forget that do so at their peril," she stated years later. "I've got pure steel up my backbone." Nobody could ever destroy me, and no one could ever ruin Johnnie as long as I could stand by his bedside—some of his family attempted to stop me—and will my life force into him."

Unfortunate Encounter

Another man later entered Diana's life, but he did so through her elder sister. Sarah, 22, met Prince Charles at a home party at Windsor Castle. Despite the fact that Sarah was extremely thin, Charles exhibited an immediate interest. He even enquired about her eating disorder. Frances had taken Sarah to the hospital because the sickness was so severe at first. Charles and Sarah appeared to have a strong attraction based on their personalities. The prince had become tired of the arrogant, frequently dull people in his circle of contacts, so he found Sarah's rebellious nature and irreverent sense of humor extremely refreshing. It didn't take long for the British media to pick up on the young couple's indiscretions. The tabloids began to publish photos of Sarah accompanying the prince to various functions. However, Charles was evidently more impressed by Sarah's other qualities than by her physical appearance. Sarah was surprised that Charles had not attempted to encourage a sexual encounter.

Diana's life was transformed in November 1977, when she took a weekend off from West Heath to see Sarah at Althorp and meet her new beau. Charles and Diana first laid eyes on each other in a plowed field near Nobottle Wood. Sarah was enraged when she learned that her sister had openly flirted with the prince. It was not unexpected that Sarah felt threatened. Diana began to blossom when she turned 16, and she became more joyful. As she shed the shyness that had bound her as a youngster, the sense of humor she had always possessed turned outward. Diana's confidence grew as her thoughts of inadequacy faded. She was no longer the girl who felt undesired because her parents desired a boy when she was born. That wound has healed over time. Her natural social abilities and genuine interest in others had always drawn people to her, and when combined with her newfound confidence, she had become the life of any party.

Diana was flattered that evening at the Althorp dance when it became clear that Charles wanted to spend time with her. She was overjoyed that she didn't have to put on a show for the prince to be interested in her. Sarah felt the polar opposite. Diana recalls Charles asking if he might see the famed Althorp picture museum that evening. Diana agreed quickly, but Sarah shoved her aside and took charge. Diana was both delighted and shocked that the prince was interested in her. She had an instinct that he was in love with her.

Diana's first relationship with Prince Charles was far from one-sided. Though she later spoke frequently about Charles's pursuit of her, others have spoken about her infatuation with him. It's reasonable that a formerly shy, insecure young woman would be enamored by a dashing young prince who showed an interest in her. Penny Walker, a West Heath piano instructor who taught Diana, remembered that her student was certainly kidnapped by the prince. Walker recalls her speaking glowingly about meeting and spending time with Charles. In fact, she remembered Diana talking about nothing else than the issue and remarking passionately on it. Walker found nothing remarkable about it, especially given Diana's age, who would be naturally delighted by such a meeting. Receiving attention from a prince, after all, is something out of a fairy tale, even for someone bred in an aristocratic family like Diana.

Jane's life was also about to alter when she married childhood friend Robert Fellowes, a 36-year-old Royal Scots Guardsman she had known growing up in Norfolk. The ceremony took place at the Guards Chapel in the Wellington Barracks, just a short distance from Buckingham Palace. Frances paid for the entire wedding, but she was second fiddle to Raine, who was preoccupied with preparing the occasion. Frances and Johnnie's tension was palpable during the wedding, which was attended by members of the royal family.

It wouldn't be the only conflict involving a Spencer family member. Sarah's reckless fostering of a conversation with the British tabloid press enraged Prince Charles, causing their relationship to end. When Sarah joined the prince to a skiing party in Switzerland in February

1978, images of the couple on the slopes appeared in the headlines. It was reported that Prince Charles has a new girlfriend. Sarah appreciated the attention and agreed to a lengthy interview with Woman's Own magazine about her connection with the prince and other topics. She discussed her drinking issue, which led to her expulsion from school. She talked about her anorexia, claiming that a physician told her she couldn't have children (she subsequently had three). She mentioned having numerous boyfriends.

Then she went on about Prince Charles, describing his romantic proclivities and his proclivity for falling in love easily. She also stated that she was not in love with him because she was not swayed by slow courtships. She went on to explain that if the two were destined to be together, she would already be engaged to Charles, and that if he did ask her, she would decline because neither of them was ready to marry. She came to the conclusion that she and the prince had a more brotherly-sisterly relationship. Though nothing Sarah said about her relationship with Charles was false, the prince was furious that she told tabloid reporters about her sentiments for him and those she believed he had for her.

While Sarah was losing favor with Charles, her parents were at a loss for what to do with Diana. Diana was only 17 when she returned from England after finishing school in Switzerland. Her contempt for Raine drew her back to Frances. Even though Frances was in Scotland, she moved in with two pals at her mother's house in Chelsea. She received the same financial support from her parents as a child. Johnnie and Frances urged her to plan for her future, but Diana lacked the necessary skills and experience to secure a job suitable for a young adult. She briefly worked as a nanny before enrolling in three-month courses in both cooking and ballet instruction, the latter of which resulted in a position teaching two-year-olds at a dance studio.

Diana's first professional job appeared to be anything but wonderful. Though she had always enjoyed dancing and working with children, she was just not prepared for a regular work routine away from family and friends. Diana was overcome by the burden of teaching toddlers to dance while their moms and nannies looked on. She abruptly quit after three months. Diana didn't leave her work because of stress alone. She had also ripped all of the tendons in her left ankle when skiing with friend Mary-Ann Stewart-Richardson in the French Alps.

Though Diana's fall down the slopes had a severe impact on her professional life, the vacation proved to be extremely eventful. Diana not only considered it one of the most delightful vacations of her young life, but she also made new friends who she would keep for the rest of her adult life. These new friendships were not with anyone in the Stewart-Richardson family, who were utilizing the ski trip to escape the somber reminders of a recent family tragedy. Diana felt uneasy staying in their chalet while they mourned, so she agreed quickly when Simon Berry, whose father had made a fortune in the wine business, invited her to join his group instead. Berry and his buddies, who had formed their own travel firm, were young and ambitious. Diana genuinely loved their company, participating in their ridiculous songs and pil-low battles. Her new classmates made fun of her when she mentioned a framed picture of Prince Charles shot in 1969 that she had prominently displayed in her dorm room. She stated it was given to her by the school.

In the years to come, Diana and Prince Charles would be the subject of even more serious discussion. But first, she needed to organize her personal and professional lives, which would necessitate some assistance from her family.

CHAPTER 4:
Crossing Paths

Diana came out of her shell socially as she reached her 18th birthday. Despite having matured significantly, she lacked confidence. Her dismal days of feeling guilty about being born a girl were over, but she still had a negative self-image. Her parents' divorce, her comparatively poor academic performance, and her early professional failures all weighed heavily on her.

Adam Russell, a deer farmer whose direct ancestors included former British Prime Minister Stanley Baldwin, was among those who befriended Diana on the ski holiday to the French Alps. Diana came to know Russell well because he, too, was confined to the chalet due to an accident sustained on the slopes. Russell had negative first impressions of Diana. Though he liked the future princess, he dug deeper and discovered a young woman who was still disturbed by her past rather than filled with hope for the future. He remembered her giggling and making a snarky remark to him when she first arrived, which turned him off. Russell regarded her as insecure, despite the fact that he believed she should have been confident. He saw Diana as a young woman who was joyful on the outside but painted on the inside by her parents' divorce after spending more time with her. Diana needs a sense of accomplishment on both a personal and professional level.

Her family's operations provided her with both. Sister Sarah, who had secured a job at Savills, a major real estate brokerage, acquired Diana a luxury apartment for her 18th birthday. Diana quickly honored a promise she made to school friend Carolyn Bar-tholomew that they would become roommates as soon as the opportunity arose. Sophie Kimball and Philippa Coaker, who worked at Savills with Sarah, moved in briefly before being replaced by Virginia Pittman and Anne Bolton. The quartet had a great time together. They spent their free time laughing and having pure pleasure. Even a burglary that cost Diana a lot of her jewelry didn't dampen Diana's enthusiasm for such youthful pastimes. Diana had a sense of pride in the apartment—her own possession—for the first time in her young adult life, despite the fact that her parents had purchased it. She used the skills she gained during her brief stint in cooking school to prepare gourmet specialties such as Russian borscht soup and chocolate roulades, however none of the four cooked whole dinners. Diana charged her housemates rent and organized a cleaning cycle among them as the landlady. She made it clear who was in control by emblazoning the words "Chief Chick" on the door to her bedroom, which was the largest in the apartment. Bartholomew recalled Diana's intense desire to have her own home, which spurred the future princess to clean it while wearing rubber gloves.

Diana discovered a position where she could thrive about this time. She got a part-time teaching job at Young England Kindergarten. She taught the children painting, sketching, and dance so well that the school's directors, Victoria Wilson and Kay Seth-Smith, added hours to her schedule. Diana also appreciated her weekly afternoon care for the small son of an American oil executive.

Diana attempted to improve her friendship with Sarah while also earning additional money by cleaning her sister's home in Chelsea. She played Cinderella by washing the floor on her hands and knees and performed numerous other domestic duties for pennies on the dollar. Sarah's roommate, Lucinda Craig Harvey, believed her roommate was taking advantage of Diana. When Harvey asked Diana to undertake basic home chores, Sarah allegedly encouraged her not to feel humiliated. Diana liked her spare time with her housemates in part because of the drudgery of such activities. They played immature pranks like calling people with unusual names they found in the phone book. They even dumped eggs and flour on the car of one of the boys who had let Diana down on a date.

There were other dates, some of whom Sarah had rejected. Diana was physically and spiritually appealing to young guys. They laughed at her often bizarre sense of humor. Diana, however, retreated when they sought to pursue the relationship further. She had a sense of destiny in her life, which translated into her remaining virgin. During Diana's marriage to Prince Charles, Bartholomew expressed her conviction that a guiding force played a role in strengthening the connection. According to Bartholomew, Diana's spiritual feeling prohibited her from allowing men to go farther physically.1 She was keeping herself "pure" for the man of her destiny, much to the chagrin of the young men who were drawn to the attractive, shapely Diana. Among them was Rory Scott, who subsequently complained that despite his attraction to the future princess, his friendship with her remained platonic. Throughout their time together, he felt a little detached from her.

Was she truly putting herself aside for Prince Charles? Such emotions would have been premature for two reasons. First and foremost, she had yet to build anything more than a friendly relationship with him. Second, he was overwhelmed by would-be queens. Some had genuine feelings for the prince, while others merely desired to wear the crown. Diana, like any other teenager in Britain at the time, looked up to the prince. She had formed a yearning to mother him after spending more than a few fleeting minutes with him. When Irish Republican Army extremists detonated a bomb that killed Earl Mountbatten, his father's uncle and life mentor with whom Charles had formed a close bond, she was very sympathetic.

The Prince's Love Life

Charles had had more than enough of the opposite sex. Lady Amanda Knatchbull, the granddaughter of the assassinated earl who had played matchmaker, was one of his suitors. Following the murder, the couple remained together, fueling talk that a wedding was on the horizon. Perhaps it would have been if Earl Mountbatten had lived long enough to see the romance through. However, Amanda rejected the idea of sacrificing her privacy as a member of the royal family, putting an end to such conjecture. However, the two remained friends for long years after that.

The same could not be true for Anna Wallace, a young Scottish woman who caught Prince Charles' attention on a foxhunting trip in late 1979. Most observers believe Amanda Knatchbull would have been welcomed with wide arms, but Wallace, who was combative and opinionated, elicited the opposite reaction. Despite this, the prince continued to date Wallace. But her obsessive attitude eventually wore off, particularly when he disregarded her during a ball celebrating the Queen Mother's 80th birthday at Windsor Castle. She was enraged when he danced with another woman that night. When he did the same thing at their next public engagement, she stormed out. She married another within a month. Camilla Parker Bowles, with whom Prince Charles had been in love for years, was the woman with whom he danced the night away on both occasions. In 1971, he was 23 years old when he met Camilla Shand. Shand, who was highly brilliant, well educated, funny, and extraordinarily attractive, drew the young prince in right away. Shand's involvement with Andrew Parker Bowles, a dashing officer in the Household Cavalry a decade older than his adversary, could have changed the course of England's royal history. He was also more serious about marrying than Prince Charles, who spent a lot of time with Camilla in 1972 but was not yet looking for a marriage.

In early 1973, the prince embarked on an eight-month cruise with the Royal Navy. Midway through his assignment, he learns Camilla had gotten engaged to Parker Bowles. That July, the pair married. Prince Charles had already shifted his focus to Knatchbull at that point. Yet, when he left the Royal Navy three years later, he was no closer to marriage than he had been at the age of 23. The prince was understandably fussy. After all, whatever he chose as his bride would become Queen of England. Such thoughts flooded over him even during a television interview in 1969. The lady he married had to be not only his soulmate, but also live up to royal standards. He informed reporters that he recognized the significance of his bride-to-be selection, which prompted him to think carefully. He reasoned that even the media would be expecting a lot from his decision. Prince Charles frequently remarked about the difference between women who actually loved him and those who put on a show in order to be queen. While friends and members of the royal family urged him to find a good marriage, he maintained that it just wasn't that simple. "My marriage has to be forever," he told Kenneth Harris in a January 7, 1975, Observer piece.

Many individuals have the erroneous impression about what love is all about. It is more than simply falling madly in love with someone and having a love affair with them for the rest of your married life. It's essentially a strong friendship. You frequently have common interests and beliefs, as well as a great degree of affection. And I believe you are really fortunate if you find the individual beautiful both physically and mentally. Marriage means a lot to me. ..It appears to be one of the most important and responsible milestones in one's life. ...Marriage is something you should work on. I may easily be proven wrong, but I aim to work on it when I marry.

Lord Mountbatten had instilled in Prince Charles a dishonest image of the ideal connection between the prince and his possible spouse. It confirmed many of Charles's preconceived beliefs about what he was looking for. "In a case like yours, I believe the man should sow his wild oats and have as many affairs as he can before settling down, but for a wife, he should choose a suitable, attractive, and sweet-characterered girl before she has met anyone else she might fall for," he wrote to Charles. "I think it's disturbing for women to have experiences if they have to remain on a pedestal after marriage."

In 1979, the prince was still looking for a perfect lifetime companion when he rekindled his romance with Camilla Parker Bowles. He poured his heart and soul out to Camilla, telling her about his worries about finding a suitable marriage, among other things. She was open to a closer relationship with the prince, especially since she suspected her husband had strayed frequently. When Andrew embarked for a six-month business trip to Rhodesia (now Zimbabwe), Camilla and the prince jumped at the chance to spend time together. They fell in love instantly, but relationships involving Prince Charles were difficult to conceal. Friends and members of the royal family told him that an affair with a married woman may damage his reputation. Andrew Parker Bowles seemed unconcerned. He didn't feel jealous as he saw the prince kiss his bride passionately on the dance floor at a polo ball in 1980.

Charles didn't necessarily want to marry, but he felt compelled to do so. The assassination of Earl Mountbatten, who had strongly believed that the prince needed to find a bride, weighed hard on his heart and mind in July 1980, when he and Diana were both invited to spend the weekend at the home of a mutual friend. Diana approached the prince on a bale of hay during a barbeque and spoke calmly about Earl Mountbatten's death and the effect she sensed it had on him. She expressed her concern about his melancholy at the funeral and stated that he needed someone to take care of him emotionally. Diana's remarks struck a chord with him. But there was another emotion she hadn't anticipated or wanted. She later said that he leaped on her, which surprised her. She was too young and inexperienced to behave otherwise. Despite her withdrawal, Charles invited her to accompany him to London the next day. He informed her of his desire to work in

Buckingham Palace, but she declined his invitation. The prince didn't appear to be trying to further his intimate relationship with Diana. He invited her to sail with him aboard his royal yacht Britannia for a week. According to Prince Charles' official biographer, Jonathan Dimbleby, he surprised a close friend by indicating that he had finally met the lady he intended to marry and commended Diana for her warmth and easygoing style. The prince felt reassured when others close to him raved about Diana. Patti Palmer-Tomkinson, whose husband Charles was one of his closest friends, was among them. Diana's cheerful personality and willingness to laugh at herself captivated Palmer-Tomkinson right away. She once fell into a swamp and was covered in mud, but instead of becoming enraged, she laughed merrily. Parker-Tomkinson noticed in her a willingness to try new things as well as a strong interest in the prince.

The blossoming affair gained traction in September, when Charles invited Diana to the Braemar Games at Balmoral, Queen Elizabeth's Highland castle retreat. Diana was overwhelmed by the royal family's social expectations. Passing such a test necessitated a significantly greater understanding of social conventions than was ever taught at West Heath. Her concerns were allayed when she discovered she would be staying in a cottage on the estate rather than the main house. Prince Charles, on the other hand, did not treat her as an afterthought. He invited her to spend daily time with him.

Diana even impressed the Queen Mother, with whom she stayed on her October visit to Scotland while Prince Charles was overseas. The fact that the Queen Mother invited Diana to spend time with her was interpreted as a hint that the royal family thought she was not just a good partner for the prince but also prospective queen material.

Fatal Addiction

Diana relished the attention, and her affections for the prince grew stronger. The media focus, on the other hand, was more than alarming. Tabloid photographers once followed the pair to a river where Charles was fishing. Unaware of the perseverance of such journalists, she scurried behind a tree in the hope that they would go. The photographers kept taking shots in an attempt to figure out who she was, but Diana concealed her face and fled through the woods.

Such ingenious means of protecting her anonymity couldn't last long. Soon, reporters were camped out in front of her flat, hoping for a sight and a word with the young woman they now regarded as the most likely contender to marry Prince Charles. They taunted her by congregating outside the Young England kindergarten. Diana was bothered by the hounding, but she never let it show to members of the press, to whom she was polite while offering no juicy details about her relationship with the prince. He and the royal family made no attempt to stem the tide, maybe because they believed such media attention was unavoidable and were interested in how Diana would manage it.

Diana was enraged because Charles seemed more concerned with Camilla's struggle than with her own difficulties. He expressed sympathy for Camilla's experience with several journalists camped outside her home, but he dismissed Diana's complaints about far bigger annoyances. Diana, on the other hand, remained silent. She'd fallen in love with the prince and didn't want to upset his plans. Despite the fact that scores of journalists were camped outside her apartment, Diana never discussed those concerns with the prince. She would have thought that having only four journalists outside her house was a quiet moment. Members of the media did not simply show up on Coleherne Court or at her workplace. Diana was followed wherever she went. She felt impelled to flee at times, which she did while driving. She frequently sped through a red light, forcing reporters who were following her to come to a halt. When she was leaving her house to join Charles at Broadlands, she escaped through the kitchen window to avoid the crowd of reporters, with whom she remained polite. She admits to crying numerous times over her situation and lamented the fact that she had no assistance from the royal family.

Diana also didn't want to make any noise about Charles's relationship with Camilla, which made her uncomfortable. Diana was perplexed as to why Camilla was privy to sensitive details about her connection with the prince. And Charles rarely invited Diana to an event without the Parker-Bowlesses accompanying her. Diana's yearning to be alone with him was frequently unsatisfied. Nonetheless, the prince demonstrated his desire for Diana as a potential wife. He took her on a tour of his Gloucestershire estate before asking her to sketch out suggestions for its interior decoration. She thought the request was a little early given that they hadn't yet gotten engaged.

Despite the prince's ongoing friendship with Camilla, the latter actively encouraged him to propose to Diana. Many acquaintances believed Camilla sought to keep a passionate presence in Charles' life and figured that marrying a young, timid woman with no experience in romance would make that easier. Diana's nagging misgivings about Charles' affections for Camilla, as well as the continual hounding by the British press, did not deter her. She blushed like a schoolgirl around the prince, whom she adored. Her excitement at being picked by the Prince of Wales was heightened by the fact that she had never had a partner.

On February 6, 1981, she became officially engaged. After returning from a skiing trip, Charles proposed to Diana. Diana laughed in response. The prince repeated his proposal, underlining its gravity by reminding her that she will one day be queen. She said that she would marry him and expressed her love for him. He then said something strange that called his affections for her into doubt. The prince replied, "Whatever love means," and went off to call the queen. These were the exact words he repeated during media interviews about the engagement.

Soon after, Diana traveled to Australia with her mother to begin preparing the wedding, but it proved to be a foreshadowing of things to come in terms of her relationship with the prince. She seemed to miss him considerably more than he seemed to miss her. He didn't return her phone calls, which she found strange and ominous.

Diana would not be the last to question Charles' feelings for her.

In fact, the problem would devastate her marriage.

CHAPTER 5:
The Relationship

Diana and Charles were both emotionally immature. Diana has minimal experience with relationships with people of the other gender. She had stayed a virgin in the hope that keeping "pure" would satisfy Charles and the royal family. The Queen Mother and others, on the other hand, had pressed Charles to marry. It is often assumed that he married Diana more out of obligation to friends and family than out of a genuine, passionate love for her.

Meanwhile, Diana's friends and most of her family were praising her as a joyful fairy tale princess, but Frances knew otherwise. She was the only person in Diana's inner circle who warned her against the marriage. She expressed her fears during a trip to Australia with her kid. Perhaps Frances saw parallels to her early friendship with Johnnie. She believed Diana was too young to marry and that the age difference between her and the prince was too significant. What would Diana think if she grew up and wanted to spread her wings and fulfill her full potential? Frances had felt exactly the same way. She didn't want Diana to make the same error she had.

During his quest for a wife, Prince Charles prioritized finding a woman whose desire to marry him surpassed her desire to be queen. Considering such a requirement, Diana was a great choice, according to her brother, who sensed her overwhelming excitement and happiness when she notified her family of the engagement the day after the prince proposed. Charles remembered his sister looking and acting overjoyed about the engagement. He also received the idea that she was confident in her ability to deal with the strong media scrutiny. Diana's Coleherne Court roommates shared her happiness. She didn't want their relationship to change. She was unwilling to change. She did, however, wish to include them in the enthusiasm.

When she found out about the engagement, she would call out to her pals, "Come quick, they're talking about us on the telly!"

That lovely honey of bliss would quickly evaporate. Diana relocated to Buckingham Palace, where she felt isolated, if not imprisoned. Despite her aristocratic upbringing and education, she felt out of place associating with the royal family and their entourage, many of whom she found stuffy and dull. Pressure was building from all sides. How would she handle the flood of media attention? How would she deal with the pressures of being a princess and eventual queen? Was her freedom and privacy forever gone? Diana was plagued by such questions. She was playing a character with little assurance. In an instant, she had gone from an unknown teenager to the main character of a fairy tale seen by the entire globe.

At this point, the sickness that had afflicted sister Sarah began to affect her as well. Diana, who was chased by young men all over London, became excruciatingly thin as a result of bulimia nervosa. During the five months between the announcement of her engagement and the wedding, her waist size shrank from 29 inches to 2312 inches. Her acquaintances couldn't help but notice. Bartholomew recalled Diana's unhappiness and weight loss upon her relocation to Buckingham Palace, both of which worried her. Diana, she realized, was just overwhelmed by the pressure from all sides. Diana struggled between eating three meals a day and having cake with her afternoon tea and slimming down for the cameras. She was scared of being a chubby princess, especially in an era when fashion models were excruciatingly thin. As a result, she cleansed her food, allowing her to satisfy everyone except herself.

Few people, especially members of the royal family, were aware of her plight. The Queen Mother had been extremely insistent about the prince proposing to Diana. Everything appeared to be fine on both sides of the family now that it was completed. Johnnie's cousin and confidante, Robert Spencer, saw nothing but acceptance and cheerful expectation. "I don't recall any reservations at the time," he stated.

> *I remember just celebrating, because it did appear then how eminently suitable Diana was. She'd never had any serious affairs, she was 19-and-a-half, extremely beautiful and most popular, and she seemed to share interests with the Prince of Wales. She gave the impression of loving the country life, in particular staying at Balmoral. She seemed to be madly in love with him and, after all, she did come from the stock of a fam-ily who had worked with and supported the Royal Family for many generations. And it seemed ever more suitable because the Prince seemed like somebody who would want a younger girl to be his wife. She was young enough to be trained, and young enough to be helped, and young enough to be molded.*[2]

People Enjoy Playing Games

Hunting was one activity that Diana and Prince Charles did not enjoy. Camilla Parker Bowles found that knowledge highly interesting for reasons unbeknownst to Diana at the time. Camilla and Diana had met for lunch shortly after the announcement of their engagement. Camilla invited the princess-to-be to the meeting while the prince was on an official tour to Australia and New Zealand. During lunchtime,

Camilla questioned Diana about her plans to accompany her husband on hunting trips. She seemed glad when Diana informed her that she had no desire to do so. Diana didn't realize Camilla was figuring out when she could have Charles all to herself until much later.

"We had lunch, and considering how immature I was, I had no idea about jealousy, depression, or anything like that," Diana recalled.

I had a wonderful existence being a kindergarten teacher—you didn't suffer from anything like that, you got tired but that was it. There was no one around to give you grief. So we had lunch. Very tricky indeed. She said, "You are not going to hunt, are you?" I said, "On what?" She said, "Horse. You are not going to hunt when you go and live at Highgrove, are you?" I said, "No." She said, "I just wanted to know" and I thought as far as she was concerned that was her communication route. Still too immature to understand all the messages coming my way.

Prince Charles was also sending messages, though not always with the best intentions. Diana overheard him telling Camilla on the phone that his love for her would never fade. Diana informed him that she had been eavesdropping at the door, resulting in a heated debate. On her first public date with Prince Charles after the engagement was announced, she wore a stunning black dress that revealed a lot of cleavage from a busty young woman, reversing her modest and meek persona. Even though such seductive attire did not fit the royal image, and black was typically reserved for mourning, Diana's message to both Charles and Camilla was apparent. It was a type of coming-out celebration, one that attempted to reveal Diana as a teenager in years only. All she could do was dress confidently. On that particular occasion, she confided in Princess Grace while visiting the powder room. Diana's misgivings were not alleviated by the reply, which was lighthearted. "Don't worry," Grace reassured her. "It will get a lot worse."

Diana had plenty of time to stew on any doubts she had about Camilla and Charles at the time. The royal family had given little thought to what role she should play other than princess. She spent much of her engagement bored as the people around her at Buckingham Palace went about their business. She felt as if her industrious and joyful life had been ripped away from her. She wasn't Diana Spencer anymore, but rather a sad captive in a fairy tale. Diana missed spending time with her friends and doing things like borrowing clothes from them and conversing about trivial matters. She was no longer in her element. The official company at Buckingham Palace, she felt, was chilly and impersonal.

In reaction, she focused her attention on the palace servants, with whom she felt a much stronger bond. Despite being reared in an aristocratic household, she had always felt more at ease around commoners. She formed a friendship with Michael Colborne, the prince's private secretary, who met Diana before the engagement and was struck by her desire to relate to him on a personal basis rather than as a potential queen of England. She inquired if she may use his given first name, and he said she could, but he could only address her as "Ma'am." The two got along great. From the engagement through the wedding, they shared an office and discussed a variety of topics. Diana was often sad when Colborne went for lunch, according to Colborne.

Diana sought to pass the time in her palatial suite, which had a bedroom, bathroom, sitting area, and a small kitchen. She was given two servants, which she hardly used. Diana passed the time by shopping and running errands for the wedding, watching soap operas, and tap dancing back in time. She felt miserably inadequate in the social graces demanded of her when she did make appearances at specific gatherings. She later complained about the palace staff's lack of training in key skills such as when to enter a room before or after the prince. That allegation was challenged by Charles' biographer Jonathan Dimbleby, who presented a quite different selection. "[Several advisors tried to] instruct her in the ways of the court and what they saw as her duties," Dimbleby recalled. "They explained that her future role as consort... would be more complicated than she had anticipated, and that her husband would not be by her side as frequently as either of them would have preferred." They also warned her that "she would always be expected to walk in his shadow."

Diana was taught the curtsy and the "royal wave," which was a raised palm cupped forward and swiveled from side to side. Prince Charles urged her to stay fresh amid a crowd by shaking hands with every sixteenth person and smiling warmly when avoiding answering a pointed question. The amount of training she received in royal etiquette, as well as how much she was required to acquire on her own, has been contested. A more mature and assured lady may have taken command of the situation, but Diana, at 19, was neither.

She was likewise hesitant to approach Charles's relationship with Camilla with confidence. The prince revealed the relationship to Diana, but assured her that she would be the only woman in his life. It's been suggested that a more trusting Diana would have encouraged his devotion. Instead, she tried in vain to persuade him to sell his Highgrove rural property, which was only 11 miles away from Camilla's.

Diana's suspicions were aroused once more just two weeks before the wedding when she opened a parcel addressed to Camilla that had been left on Colborne's desk. Despite the prince's confidential secretary's concerns, she opened it and saw a bracelet with the initials G. F., which she recognized as Charles's nickname for Camilla: "Girl Friday." Diana sobbed her way out of the office. She confronted Charles, who informed her that it was a gift for Camilla to be given during a lunch commemorating their separation on July 27, two days before the wedding. Diana, on the other hand, suspected that Camilla and the prince would not say farewell. While Charles was dining with Camilla, Diana was having lunch with her sisters, who informed her that it was too late to cancel the wedding.

Diana looked for sympathetic ears throughout the engagement. One of them was Queen Elizabeth II, who thoroughly loved her company and readily agreed to dine with her on a regular basis. "Will the

Queen be dining alone today?" Diana would call a staff member and ask timidly. When she was notified of the request, the queen would always respond, "Oh, do ask her to join me." Diana's sentiments for Queen Elizabeth II evolved from royal reverence to genuine affection, especially because she was always accommodating during difficult times. Diana saw in Queen Elizabeth a lady who had adapted to the hardships and procedures of royalty, just as she would have to. And it looked that the queen was more confident in Diana's ability to make that move than her son was.

Even the most basic activities produced a commotion. Diana went for a brief walk one weekend day, and all hell broke loose due to security worries. She told Colborne about it the next Monday, and he offered her plenty of forewarning about her destiny as Princess of Wales. "This is going to be your life," remarked Colborne. "You'll never be on your own again." And you will transform. You'll be an awful b*tch in four to five years, not through any fault of your own, but because of the circumstances in which you live. You can eat four boiled eggs for breakfast if you wish. If you need the automobile carried around to the front door right now, you'll get it. It will alter your life."

Purging and Binging

Diana's bulimia was exacerbated by the great stress she felt as the wedding approached. It wasn't until much later that she realized why she was overeating and purging. The stress was only one aspect of it. "When you have bulimia, you're very ashamed of yourself and hate yourself, so—and people think you're wasting food, so you don't discuss it with people," Diana explained. "The thing about bulimia is that your weight never changes, whereas with anorexia you visibly shrink." So (with bulimia) you may pretend the entire time. There is no evidence." Nonetheless, there was proof. Diana shed 14 pounds in the four months before the nuptials. She admitted herself, "I had shrunk to nothing."8 Diana wasn't just bulimic, which was one of the reasons for her weight reduction. Her concern with her attractiveness led to multiple fasting episodes. Though her bulimia was more severe, her general unhealthy eating habits induced by both her stress and her still-poor self-image had a significant influence in her weight loss.

Despite spending more time with Diana during the engagement than she had in several years and being aware of her daughter's bulimia, Frances chose not to become involved. Diana's mother had her own eating disorders and was aware of Sarah's episodes with bulimia. Fran-ces has been chastised for her lack of concern for Diana's concerns at the time. She confessed that she recognized her daughter's eating disorder right away, owing to her own experience with the sickness. But she didn't want to become too involved for fear of exacerbating and even exacerbating the problem.

Diana was lonely. Her family members were giddy with excitement about their potential ties with the royal family, but Sarah remained resentful of her for marrying a guy with whom she had previously been connected. Diana had lost touch with her Coleherne Court acquaintances. She had no one to whom she could confess her worries. Raine and Johnnie talked glowingly about Diana to the press. They extolled her ability to quickly transition into the role of princess. Diana hadn't told them about her greatest worries, so some of her optimism could have been a whistle in the dark.

Her dual public character was on display in two public appearances just before the wedding. The first was a royal ball hosted by Charles at Buckingham Palace for family and guests. Diana appeared to be in good spirits during the joyful evening, however she claimed to be an emotional wreck as the ceremony approached. She spent a lot of time dancing with young guys she had met at Coleherne Court, such as Rory Scott. Her anxiety was palpable when she arrived at Windsor

Great Park to watch Charles play polo—their final public appearance together before the wedding. There were 20,000 people in attendance, many of whom came to see his bride-to-be rather than the prince swinging the royal mallet. It was not a promising sight. On July 27, 1981, John Edwards of the Daily Mirror wrote, "Her face was pale and gray as limestone, and she hardly smiled." She dashed out of Prince Charles' open Aston Martin before it had even stopped. She rushed immediately to the Queen's private cabin, twisting a white cardigan in her hands, looking nervously from behind the door at the masses and refusing to join them. She appeared to have altered in a matter of days. Her springiness had vanished. The quips remained buried. She had lost weight and was nervous by the crush all around her."

Although Diana felt she had no control over her fate, she kept a semblance of control by disregarding Charles' desires and hiring her own dressmakers for the big event. They were David and Elizabeth Emanuel, a young couple with little expertise in the arts, especially in constructing a masterpiece for one of history's most renowned marriages. Diana reasoned that if the fairy story didn't proceed as planned, the historical attire would fit the fairy tale concept. She also had the Emanu-els sew a diamond-encrusted horseshoe into her waistline for good luck. Diana insisted on puffy sleeves, floating silk, and a 25-foot taffeta train adorned with sequins and pearls. As her father accompanied her down the aisle, she imagined the flowery dress whisking her from her painful existence into a realm of love and optimism.

Despite Diana's claims of being sick after a bulimic episode on the eve of the wedding, others close to her recounted a quite different narrative. Among them was William Tallon, the Queen Mother's elderly page. Tallon perceived Diana as lively, enthusiastic, and joyful when he welcomed her into his office for a nice discussion. "She saw my bike against a wall and got on it and started riding around and round," Tallon recounted. "(She was) ringing the bell while singing, 'I'm marrying the Prince of Wales tomorrow.'" Ring, ring, ring. 'I'm being married to the Prince of Wales tomorrow!' Ring, ring, ring! I can hear the bell on that bicycle now. She was just a child, a small girl, you know." Diana, on the other hand, became an expert at masking her sadness. She admits to breaking down at the wedding rehearsal in St. Paul's Cathedral, but the tears must have been shed privately, because friends and family members didn't notice anything wrong. Diana did admit to crumbling emotionally during the engagement due to her jealousy and mistrust of Camilla and her inability to deal with it. Yet, Sarah Jane Gaselee, an 11-year-old bridesmaid, believed Diana was experiencing quite the opposite while seeing the soon-to-be princess at the rehearsal supper. "I don't think she was stressed by it or anything," Gaselee said years later. "It didn't happen like that. What I do remember is that, as best as I could tell, she and Charles were madly in love at the time. I observed them embracing on the sofa, and during rehearsals, their arms were linked and they were skipping down the aisles. "I thought it was all very happy."

Diana appeared to be comforted at the moment by a symbol of love she received from Charles on the day she spent at Clarence House. The prince sent her a signet ring with the Prince of Wales feathers etched on it, along with a note that said, "I'm so proud of you, and when you come up, I'll be there at the altar for you tomorrow." Just stare them in the eyes and knock 'em out." Though such a message was devoid of romance and feelings of love, it helped soothe Diana. But she was too composed. The reality of her circumstances had numbed her. Diana described herself as a vulnerable lamb on its way to slaughter.

Diana awakened early on her wedding day, July 29, 1981, to the celebratory sounds of a large crowd assembled outside Clarence House. She remembered a scene from the movie The Graduate in which the bride bolted down the aisle and ran out of the church. When the wedding bells rung, would she still feel like a lamb on its way to slaughter? Or will she fall in love with Charles and be overcome with hope? Even she had no idea while the entire world anticipated the Wedding of the Century.

CHAPTER 6:
The Marriage

Diana was under a lot of stress in the run-up to the wedding. However, the outside variables would have made anyone anxious. After all, it was to be a worldwide event at the revered St. Paul's Cathedral. Not only were 3,500 individuals invited, but 2 million people lined the ceremonial route, overwhelming Diana and her father. Another 750 million people watched the wedding on television throughout the world. When radio listeners are included, the total number of people tuned in is close to a billion. Diana's aspirations stretched beyond her role as a fairy tale princess for a day. She was to be the first British citizen since the 1600s to marry an heir to the throne.

Diana's mind was filled with conflicting thoughts throughout her wedding day, which she began by watching television coverage of the large crowd outside. The Emanuels clothed her in her ivory silk gown and tiara before she went for Buckingham Palace, where Diana and Johnnie would be whisked away to St. Paul's Cathedral by a glass coach. Her 25-foot train had to be balanced on her lap. The fairy tale day had begun, and she was relishing every second of it.

The large throng outside Buckingham Palace produced an atmosphere of anticipation for Prince Charles. He took in the sight of 150 Union Jack flags adorning the mall poles and flowers adorning the lampposts. Every structure in sight had flags and bunting in red, white, and blue. The mob gathered in front of Buckingham Palace, cheering at each sign of life. A parade of black limousines bringing royal family members from all around the world began to make its way toward St. Paul's Cathedral. Diana and Johnnie, meanwhile, waved warmly as they drove through the masses clogging the parade route. People threw flowers at the carriage or screamed congratulations as she passed. The clamor became so loud and distracting that Johnnie mistakenly mistook St. Martin-in-the-Fields Cathedral in Trafalgar Square for St. Paul's and nearly crashed the coach. Only Diana's rapid reflexes, which pulled her father back, kept him from fleeing. Diana was overjoyed by the ecstatic reaction of her fellow Britons. Their smiles were contagious. She felt a connection to the people and hope for the future. Throughout the engagement, she had believed that her importance as a princess would be as a link to the public, rather than as a figurehead or emblem of the royal family. Many teenage girls and ladies had already adopted her haircut and outfit style.

The Emanuels rushed to spread out Diana's wrinkled train after she emerged from the coach in front of the cathedral. As she moved up the carpeted steps, it flowed smoothly. "She was extremely gentle, very shy, and she was someone that as a young girl you thought was everything a princess should be," India Hicks, a 10-year-old bridesmaid at the time, recalled. "She was very beautiful, very young, very calm—but there was a nervousness about her." But the atmosphere inside the cathedral was incredible. It's a relatively empty place, but it's full of warmth and excitement."

Diana took her time walking down the aisle, aware of her father's frail physical condition. Camilla, who was wearing a pale gray, veiled pillbox hat, was one of the guests she saw. Diana had made sure Camilla was not invited to the post-wedding luncheon, so it was the only time she saw Camilla that day. Diana was no longer enraged or envious, believing that Camilla and Charles's romantic connection was gone. Love poured over her as she approached the prince at the altar. "I remember being so in love with my husband that I couldn't take my eyes off him," Diana said. "I just absolutely thought I was the luckiest girl in the world," he said to Diana, who responded softly, "Beautiful for you."

Years later, Diana shared an entirely different memory of her emotions. Her words help explain the conflicting emotions racing through her mind: "The day I walked down the aisle at St. Paul's Cathedral, I felt that my personality had been taken away from me, and I had been taken over by the royal machine." Those words could have been a product of Diana's bitterness following the end of her relationship with Charles. On her wedding day, there was little doubt that she had a great love for her spouse and a strong feeling of optimism for the future. Later, on the Buckingham Palace balcony, she planted a kiss on Charles' lips, eliciting a cry of approbation from the large, admiring throng.

There will be no Heavenly Honeymoon.

Diana was ready to get away from the cheering crowds, flashing cameras, and media requests by the end of the day. She yearned to be alone with Prince Charles, and she thought she'd get her wish on a two-week Mediterranean honeymoon vacation on his royal yacht Brittania. She would no longer have to compete with his work schedule. The press would no longer disrupt her time with him. She simply couldn't wait any longer.

But her fairy-tale honeymoon, being alone with her husband, and simply feeling happy were all destroyed. The pair traveled to Broadlands, Lord Mountbatten's estate. All of her fears and anxiety from the engagement returned throughout the honeymoon. The permanence of her condition overwhelmed her. During a luncheon with Egyptian President Anwar Sadat, she observed Charles wearing cufflinks with entwined Cs (which stood for Charles and Camilla) that Camilla had given him in defiance of Diana's wishes, which enraged and depressed her even more. Her lack of experience as a lover, combined with her perception of his incapacity, if not unwillingness, to please her, left them both romantically yearning.

Princess Diana bemoaned that she had entered her marriage with hope, but that hope had vanished after only a few days. She grumbled about having to entertain the Brittania's crew, which left her with little time to spend with Charles. She was having horrific bulimic episodes multiple times a day, eating everything she could and then purging minutes later. She remembered crying frequently on her honeymoon and being exhausted for all the wrong reasons.

After disembarking from the yacht, the pair went straight to their destination. They were greeted warmly, although Diana later recalled a more distinct remembrance of horrific dreams starring Camilla. Her mistrust of her husband and Camilla had reached a boiling point. She felt like an untouchable figure at Balmoral, and she recalls the staff treating her with child gloves. Diana merely desired to be treated like the young lady she knew she was, rather than as a glass doll. Her jealousy of Camilla was understandable—even before she noticed the cufflinks on Charles, two images of Camilla fell out of his diary when he and Diana were reading it. She began to cry, pleading with him to tell her the truth about his affections for Camilla. He ignored their requests.

During their honeymoon, Diana and Charles revealed a personality and interest mismatch. The large age difference did as well. The prince preferred to spend his time fishing or reading. Authors such as mystical philosopher Laurens van der Post and psychotherapist Carl Jung provided him with intellectual stimulation. He tried to share his fascination with both with Diana, but she wasn't cognitively or emotionally prepared to absorb the information. Some assume that her bad academic record resulted in a low intellectual self-image. Diana, on the other hand, spent the majority of her time with the crew, with whom she had more fun. She even surprised the sailors with an impromptu piano performance. Diana would have loved to spend more time with her new husband, but Charles hoped she would take an interest in what he liked. Diana felt rejected when it became clear that he wasn't going to offer her his complete attention. In the meantime, her weight had decreased to 110 pounds.

She began to see the wisdom in her mother's warnings. In both viewpoint and age, Frances always felt much younger than Johnnie. She had married too young and had grown impatient to go her own way. Diana wasn't old enough or had been with Charles long enough to have lost her emotional relationship to him, but she was feeling the impact of their attitudes and ages. Her ennui had become apparent early in the journey. She was a young woman who liked the sun and the ocean, but these pastimes were not permitted on the boat. When they arrived at their destinations, luminaries such as Sadat occupied their time. Diana would have wanted to go shopping, but the throng prevented her from doing so. As a result, she sought entertainment wherever she could. While Charles was reading a book on the deck, she appeared unexpectedly and surprisingly to party with the crewmen, who were perplexed as to what she was doing there. Charles and Diana couldn't identify with each other. It was a mismatch from the outset, as both parties were painfully aware. "Diana dashes about chatting up all the sailors and cooks in the galley, etc., while I remain hermit-like on the verandah deck, sunk with pure joy into one of Laurens van der Post's books," Charles wrote from Brittania to friends.

Charles was both scared and annoyed by Diana's misery. He had no responses. He begged her to cheer up, but she refused. She wanted him nearby, but staying close to his unhappy wife wasn't his idea of fun, and it didn't appear to be helping. She felt abandoned when he left her alone. Charles felt sad for her, but in his life, he had always loved powerful women. Diana's flaws only served to keep his affections for her from growing. He felt smothered by her emotional needs and couldn't tell her the truth—that he loved her unreservedly.

Diana found the month at Balmoral, which finished the honeymoon, to be simply awful. She had previously spent time with the royal family, but not for such an extended amount of time. The 20-year-old princess was bored stiff throughout dinner, listening to endless anecdotes from elderly relatives, or hearing Princess Margaret sing ancient show tunes on the piano, or being thrown out of the room so the men could enjoy talk and cigars. And, as difficult as it was for Diana to adjust to life in the royal family, her behavior baffled them as well. They mistakenly assumed she was well-versed in social graces. After all, even if she was not raised in monarchy, she was raised in aristocracy. They didn't realize, however, that Diana's only exposure to such topics was at school. John-nie Spencer was not one to practice good manners; he didn't even eat dinner with his children. Raine's stuffy gatherings were either avoided or discouraged from being attended by the children.

During her month in Balmoral, Diana frequently left the dinner table without explanation or refused to come down for meals at all, which was regarded highly disrespectful in the conventional and staid realm of British royalty. Such apparent defiance in the presence of the queen was perplexing and improper. However, perplexing and unacceptable might equally define Charles' initial reaction to married life. It only took him two days on the Brittania to phone Camilla and seek her counsel. "The Prince simply had to be in constant contact with Camilla, or he couldn't function properly," attendant Stephen Barry explained. "He would become irritable and ill-tempered if he did not receive his daily phone call."

Diana urged him to take her back to London, which didn't help matters. She had mentioned a year before that Balmoral was her favorite place in the world. After the engagement was announced, she told an interviewer that one thing she and the prince had in common was a love of country. She was now describing it as "wet and boring." Charles tried to explain to her that the royal family was currently at Balmoral and that her new duty was to accompany them.

A Deficit of Chemistry

Diana had saved up for marriage with the intention of waiting for that unique moment with a special guy, but her honeymoon with Charles proved unsatisfactory. It was a shared sentiment. Diana's expectations of her first sexual encounter may have exceeded reality. However, the letdown on their wedding night had a huge influence in their lack of enthusiasm for each other over their honeymoon. "I had read all that stuff about being swept away and the earth moving, but it wasn't like that at all," Diana recounted. "It was over in an instant." 'Is that it?' I wondered as I laid there. Is this truly the big thing that everyone is making it out to be?'All he wanted was to jump my bones. Roll on, roll off, go to sleep.`` Prince Charles was similarly dissatisfied, telling associates that her inexperience left him wanting and that her bulimia purging turned him off. As a result, Charles and Diana rarely made love during their honeymoon.

By October, the relationship had deteriorated to the point where Charles asked assistant Michael Colborne to come to Balmoral and look for Diana for a while. Diana had specifically requested Colborne, who had been quite supportive of her throughout the engagement. Colborne was astounded to see how skinny she had become when he arrived. And instead of spending a couple of hours with her at a time, he found himself observing her in mute misery or listening to her tirades for three times that amount of time. She sobbed to Colborne that she'd reached the end of her rope. That was one sentiment on which she and Charles agreed, and Colborne was once again caught in the middle. Colborne overheard the pair quarrel heatedly on multiple occasions, including one when he entered the room just in time to collect Diana's wedding ring, which Charles hurled to him. In a snarky remark to Diana's declining physique, Charles requested Colborne to have the ring resized.

The prince looked to require Colborne as a sounding board and adviser as well. Charles confided in him about Diana's possessiveness and her rejection of country life. What he didn't say was that she was envious of Camilla. Many royal family members and associates believe Diana's preoccupation with Camilla eventually drove the prince into her arms. Others argue that any newlywed would have been outraged if her spouse had continued to communicate with his mistress. Diana intuitively recognized that his feelings for Camilla would always keep him from loving her unconditionally.

Diana was granted her demand to be taken to London shortly after, but not for the reasons she had hoped. Diana was referred to a psychotherapist after Charles and the queen determined she needed professional help. The royal family had usually avoided such measures, believing that Diana was simply experiencing post-wedding nerves, therefore engaging a professional signified great concern. Diana later revealed that she had seen multiple therapists and pharmacologists who had prescribed powerful medications that she refused to take. Furthermore, she suppressed medical information such as her bulimia episodes, which would have been vital to any treatment plan. Whether she was being stubborn or her point of view was valid, Diana believed she was the same lady she had always been and that she would eventually adjust to her life as a member of the royal family. She described a continuous string of analysts and psychiatrists attempting to figure out what made her tick and attempting to give Valium and other medications when she believed all she needed was time and patience. Diana believed the professionals were willing to prescribe drugs only to avert a violent episode.

Thankfully, the honeymoon ended in mid-October. Because neither Highgrove nor their Kensington Palace apartments were ready for them, the couple was compelled to relocate to Charles' previous residence in Buckingham Palace. Charles and Diana's marriage had a rocky start.

Actually, one eventuality could have exacerbated matters: Diana becoming pregnant with a child neither she nor Charles desired. So when she found out she was pregnant as her honeymoon was coming to an end, calamity could have ensued. However, it had the opposite effect, at least temporarily. Preparing for motherhood allowed her to occupy both her mind and her time. The prince was equally hopeful that the pregnancy would help his wife.

The Popular Vote

Later that month, the couple traveled to their home principality of Wales. Diana's capacity to relate to others shined through even if she didn't look good. She showed affection for the people, who returned her affection. Jayne Fincher, a freelance photographer, recalls her reaching deep into the crowd to touch people rather than using the delicate royal handshake. She contrasted Diana's outgoing and personal demeanor with the queen's dignified, formal demeanor toward commoners. Fincher recalled the queen gracefully accepting flowers with her white-gloved hand outstretched. Diana, on the other hand, wore no gloves and eagerly groped for flowers.

Those who thought "Dianamania" would die away after the wedding were mistaken. Crowds swarmed her during public appearances and were similarly huge and enthusiastic. This created an issue for Charles, who was being overshadowed. During the way to Wales, he wanted to welcome people on the other side of the road, so he switched sides with Diana. The groan of individuals who had hoped to see Diana on that side of the street was audible and embarrassing to Charles. He first accepted the wishes of the audience and smiled as he collected flowers for his wife. But as it became clear that the crowds had only come to see her, he became enraged. "She's right over there!"When the throng asked to see Diana, he would bark. "Would you like your money back?"" Charles told a Buckingham Palace official that people were not interested in seeing him. He questioned himself. After all, he was the Prince of Wales. When Diana was resting, Charles would make addresses in different parts of the principality, and press attention was minimal.

Diana was sympathetic to her husband's suffering. She requested those in charge of such events if crowds on Prince Charles' side of the road could be increased, but one cannot affect a people's emotions. Diana was aware that the prince's ego had been gravely hurt, but she saw no other option. Wales was his domain. Its Caernarvon Castle had hosted his Coming of Age ceremony 12 years before, which had been widely broadcast across the country. Now he was being upstaged by a woman he had never met a year before. "If you're a man, like my husband, a proud man, you mind about that if you hear it every day for four weeks," Diana told British Broadcasting Corporation interviewer Martin Bashir about the apparent power shift in the relationship years later. "And you feel low about it, instead of feeling happy and sharing it." The royal family felt the same way. Diana had hoped for words of encouragement for her popularity and performance in Wales, but all she got was quiet. Some feel this was because the royal family simply thought she was performing her duty. After the tour, she told longtime friend James Colthurst that she received an angry answer from Charles.

Soon after, the queen experienced Dianamania, which culminated at the State Opening of Parliament on November 4, 1981. The annual event is intended to give Her Majesty a spotlight moment. She is photographed wearing the Imperial State Crown, which bears the gleaming Black Prince's ruby, while sitting on a throne in the House of Lords. The event includes a lot of hoopla, including trumpets blaring. Members of the House of Commons are paying close attention to the Queen's speech. The occasion serves as a reminder that, despite her lack of influence in modern times, the queen remains an important figure. Nonetheless, she was not the most popular figure on that day, or any other State Opening of Parliament in the next decade. That honor belonged to Diana, who took over the show against her will. Everyone in the room was staring at Diana as she emerged from the glass vehicle that had taken her from Westminster to the House of Lords. The crowds were also curious about what she would be wearing, as she had dressed inappropriately at a prior function to take Charles' attention away from Camilla. She chose a modest white chiffon gown with a tiara and pearl choker for this occasion. Her youth and beauty diverted attention away from Queen Elizabeth II, who is 55 years old.

A photograph taken that evening of Diana fast asleep on the crimson velvet throne given by the Victoria and Albert Museum so she could sit next to Prince Charles did as well. The next day, the image emerged in newspapers all across the world, and was misinterpreted as one of a tired princess rather than a bored one. Her pregnancy became public knowledge very quickly. Barbara Cartland, step grandmother, leaked the story to the Daily Express. "The first child should be conceived in the midst of romance!"" she exclaimed. "This child will be a triumph over the heinous modern practice of postponing a family until one or both partners' careers are established." Delaying a first kid is a huge mistake. It is tampering with nature, and nature is always right. I'm hoping for a boy because that's what every Englishman and woman wants."

True, romance is in full bloom! The child was conceived on a rather unromantic honeymoon by a couple whose deep love for each other had been called into question. Diana was still physically ill, emotionally exhausted, unhappily married, and expecting a child. It was a recipe for additional strife between her and Prince Charles, as well as a worsening depression for the princess.

CHAPTER 7: Early Life as a Royal

Though rumors of a less-than-ideal relationship between Charles and Diana surfaced from time to time in the media, most believed that the fairy tale wedding had given way to a marriage with a happy ending.

That could not be farther from the truth. When the couple returned to London at the end of October, they moved into a tiny apartment on the upper level of Buckingham Palace, which included a bedroom, sitting room, bathroom, and two dressing rooms but no kitchen. Diana couldn't even make herself a cup of coffee, let alone a small breakfast or lunch. Charles didn't give the inconveniences much attention. He had grown up in Buckingham Palace and had become accustomed to having everything done for him, even meal preparation. Diana, on the other hand, relished the occasional household job. It gave her a sense of purpose.

She did, however, feel lonely. While the prince moved everywhere in his official position, she did not. She would call friends just to hear their voices. She accompanied her husband to different activities, but she was upset about her lack of influence and the amount of time she spent alone. She couldn't figure out why Charles couldn't enjoy more than a few fleeting minutes with her. She desired to be passionately loved by a husband who was more loyal to her than to his position. It was too much to ask of Prince Charles, but she was correct in questioning whether he actually loved her.

Her physical, mental, and emotional status were all harmed by her pregnancy. Every day she felt unwell. It became impossible to tell the difference between bulimia and morning sickness. Diana even postponed a visit to Bristol in mid-November due to her illness, despite her responsibility as a princess, who, after all, was meant to keep a stiff upper lip.

Diana's decision to have a baby so early in her life and marriage has sparked much debate. She searched for methods to pass the time and wanted to contribute to the preservation of British customs. After all, a son would be the heir apparent to the throne. Diana also believed that bringing a kid into the royal family's realm was the most effective method to create a positive relationship with Charles and the royal family. However, one consultant gynecologist at a London hospital suggested that Diana's timing in becoming pregnant would be bad. "I always tell women that if they don't want things to go wrong, the two things they shouldn't do are get themselves exhausted or under too much strain," he was quoted as saying in an article published in News of the World. "The Princess is constantly in the public eye, which we know causes stress because she collapsed in tears at a polo match just before the wedding."

The media hounding of Diana escalated during that tense period, and she was exceedingly self-conscious. She wasn't extremely vain, but she was driven by the desire to preserve a positive self-image. Diana was surrounded by photographers who snapped multiple images of her that appeared in publications the next day as she performed a simple errand to a neighborhood sweet store in December. Finally, the royal family stepped in. Michael Shea, the queen's press secretary, summoned members of the media to Buckingham Palace. They were told to give the princess some space. Both the Queen and the Duke of Edinburgh spoke briefly to them. They reminded reporters that Diana was not reared in a family accustomed to such attention, and that the media's relentless scrutiny and oppressive daily routine was wearing on her. When a reporter asked why Diana didn't just send a footman to the candy shop, the queen retorted angrily, "Do you know, I think that's the most pompous remark I've ever heard in my life."

Aside from the long-awaited show of support, the requests were mostly ignored by members of the media, who were neither inclined nor willing to bend to the royal family's urgings. Though the relentless tabloid coverage of Diana slowed for a brief period, the princess's overzealous treatment by the mainstream media, particularly the tabloid media, was to remain a persistent cause of irritation and sadness for the rest of her life.

Diana did get a small reprieve from her anguish during the 1981 holiday season. She was able to flee to Windsor with Charles, where she felt a lot more comfortable and pleasant. He presented her with an emerald-and-diamond ring, which she conceded captivated her. Charles wrote to a friend about their joyous celebration of their first Christmas together. He hoped that the 1982 holiday season would be much more joyous with a newborn baby to share.

Reaching Rock Bottom

The joy of the holiday season was only ephemeral. Diana's plight reappeared after the New Year. The pair was on a visit to Sandringham, where Charles spent a lot of time hunting, which Diana despised. Her emotional state had deteriorated to the point where she considered suicide. It got to the point that she flung herself down the stairs in January. She stated it was not a suicide attempt, but rather an attempt to emphasize her emotions of helplessness. "Charles said I was crying wolf," Diana remembered, "and I told him I was desperate and crying my eyes out, and he said, 'I'm not going to listen.'" You do this to me all the time. 'I'm going riding now,' I said as I hurled myself down the stairs. The Queen emerged, shocked and shaking—she was so terrified. I knew I wasn't going to lose the baby, even though I was bruised all over. Charles went out riding, and when he returned, it was just dismissed, entire dismissal."3 The incident's details were hazy. Others believe Diana informed a staff member she simply slipped and fell down the steps and was surprised to learn the queen had witnessed it. According to reports, Charles even summoned a doctor, whose examination revealed no harm to Diana or the baby. In either event, Diana's sense of urgency at the time cannot be denied.

Diana's episodes of depression elicited emotions ranging from pity and resentment toward Charles for his perceived mistreatment of his wife to a critical cry for her to pull herself together for the benefit of herself, the royal family, and the baby. Some thought her calls for help were only self-pity. After all, from the outside looking in, being married to the Prince of Wales, spending time at historic buildings like Buckingham Palace, and being waited on hand and foot do not constitute as terrible experiences in the perspective of most people. Diana, on the other hand, was unable to shake it. Her melancholy grew worse as her pregnancy progressed. In early 1982, she and Charles traveled to Windermere Island in the Bahamas for what was called a second honeymoon. Diana simply hoped it could have been done in private, because the British tabloid press was all over it. They photographed Diana in a bikini, five months pregnant—the tabloids had added sexuality to their list of reasons for their fascination with her. One Sun headline shouted, "carefree Di threw royal caution to the winds to wear her revealing outfit." She couldn't even find privacy in a secluded location 3,000 miles away from home. Both the queen and Diana were enraged at the images. The latter had always been overwhelmed by media attention, but had previously recognized the importance of their work to some extent. The photos of her racing about the Bahamas in a bikini were a watershed moment in her relationship with the tabloid press. She saw no cause for such an invasion of her privacy.

In the Bahamas, she uncovered yet another issue. The couple was staying with Charles's close friends Penny and Norton Romsey, with whom he had shared his and Diana's marital problems. They were among the most strident of those attempting to persuade Diana to stop her self-pity. Though she had had a good time in the Bahamas and had finally had time alone with Charles, she became enraged when he walked off by himself to read or paint, and she loudly complained about being bored. Diana suspected her husband had taken her to the Bahamas not for a second honeymoon, but so that his pals might prey on her.

She was further burdened by "The Diana Watch" in the media, which speculated on a daily basis on when the future king would be born. Against the recommendation of her gynecologist, George Pinker, who favored a more natural method, she chose to have her labor induced. Diana delivered delivery sooner than expected, but the labor was long and painful. It took 16 hours, during which time Diana was given an epidural injection to help her discomfort and a cesarean section was contemplated. But on June 21, 1982, at 9:03 p.m., William was born, and a nation rejoiced. Diana had given birth to an heir to the monarchy, Prince Charles' firstborn son, and a grandson for the queen.

Her eating disorder briefly subsided as a result of her excitement about childbirth. Carolyn Bartholomew, a friend who visited Diana at Kensington Palace three days after William's birth, remarked on Diana's enthusiasm for herself and her child. Diana exuded a contentment that Bartholomew hadn't seen in a long time. Diana shared Diana's sentiments. "It was a great relief because everything was peaceful again," Diana said years later. "And I was well for a time."5 So was Charles, who spoke glowingly about the experience of becoming a father to the media and family members. Throughout Diana's arduous labor, he had remained by her side. Having a kid together allowed them to form a bond, despite the fact that it was only a temporary solution to their marital troubles. "The arrival of our small son has been an astonishing experience, and one that has meant more to me than I could ever have imagined," Charles wrote to godmother Patricia Mountbatten in a letter. "I am SO thankful I was beside Diana's bedside the whole time because I really felt as though I'd shared deeply in the process of birth and as a result was rewarded by seeing a small creature which belonged to US even though he seemed to belong to everyone else as well." After William's birth, the new parents moved into their London home of Kensington Palace, which was finally ready. The weeks that followed were among Diana's happiest as Princess of Wales. Princess Margaret hosted a lively reception for the pair. Diana was satisfied that she had fulfilled her responsibilities to the throne. She soon began to feel the consequences of postpartum depression, as well as panic episodes when Charles was late arriving home. She had a deep feeling of abandonment. Outsiders might have thought she should have been celebrating her 21st birthday in July with excitement because her life appeared to be complete, but the aftereffects of delivery dampened her spirits. Diana's behavior had become unpredictable, even by her own admission. Her bulimia was affecting her mood, but she was also developing sleeplessness. During the annual royal family vacation in Balmoral, she went three nights without sleeping while binging and purging. Her weight plummeted precipitously. There is still debate over whether the royal family was aware of her eating condition.

Her Once More

Camilla, as always, was there. Diana once eavesdropped on her husband when he was on the phone with a close acquaintance. Diana overheard Charles add, "Whatever happens, I will always love you."7 Charles stated to author Jonathan Dimbleby that he had virtually little contact with Camilla for the next five years after their engagement. The only exceptions were at various social gatherings. He also stated that he only spoke to Camilla once during his marriage, and that was to inform her that Diana was pregnant. Charles told Dimbleby that he had not spoken to Camilla since William's birth until he rekindled his friendship with her in 1986. Those who claim that Charles frequently saw Camilla during fox hunting outings refute this claim. Others have said that the press spotted Charles and Camilla riding side by side at an event shortly after their trip to Wales, but did not report the news since the fairy tale component of the royal marriage was still fresh in the public's mind. Whatever the reality of Charles's relationship with Camilla during the early years of his marriage, Diana's anxieties were undoubtedly heightened.

Her misgivings of Charles, combined with the grandeur of her position as Princess of Wales, contributed to her despair. However, the prince, maybe overthinking the situation, believed that severe psychoanalysis was the solution. Laurens van der Post, whose writings he consumed on his honeymoon, was summoned. Van der Post, 80, was a fascinating man who had survived a Japanese prisoner-of-war camp during WWII and had lived among the Kalahari Bushmen of Africa. But his ability to connect with Diana, 21, was dubious at best. He suggested Diana see Dr. Alan McGlashan, a psychiatrist in London. Diana remarked that Dr. McGlashan was not only nearly as elderly as van der Post, but also was far too preoccupied with dissecting her dreams. Diana, however, opted to seek out Dr. David Mitchell since she felt she had been OK before becoming engaged to Charles. She spoke with him every night at Kensington Palace. Mitchell discussed her connection with Charles, which she saw as a major source of the problem, as well as the loss of the carefree living she had as a more typical young lady in London. But she didn't tell Mitch-ell or any professional analyst about her bulimia, which had clearly harmed her mental state since the wedding.

Diana was able to conceal her distress in public. One such instance came in late September 1982, when Diana traveled to Monaco for the funeral of Princess Grace, who died from injuries sustained in a vehicle accident—a foreshadowing of Diana's own tragic end. Diana was the perfect fit for the occasion. Monaco is recognized as a mecca of elegance and luxury, which she absolutely fit, and this was an occasion that demanded tact and sympathy, both of which she possessed in spades. Diana was favorably greeted and applauded for her appearance in Monaco. But, like she had done when she stole the show in Wales, she wasn't about to elicit even the tiniest positive reaction from the royal family.

"Look at the papers," an aide advised her the day she returned from Monaco. "They say you did brilliantly."

"Good," she said. "Because nobody ever mentioned it here."

The royal family felt it should not have been mentioned. It does not consider Princess Diana or any of its other members to be entertainers. They represent the United Kingdom and the royal family on official visits such as the one to Monaco, and they should not be praised for doing so. And therein lies the issue. Diana had just finished her adolescence and was extremely sensitive at the moment. She wished to be appreciated by Charles and the royal family, but this did not happen.

The frantic reaction to Diana had another negative effect on her marriage through no fault of her own—it made Charles envious. He had no intention of playing second fiddle to Diana when he married her. During a trip to Australia and New Zealand in March 1983, Daily Mirror photographer Kent Gavin stated that 92 of the approximately 200 photographers there focused on Diana. The crowds that were around her were fantastic. Brisbane's streets were clogged by an estimated 300,000 people. The similar frenzy followed her to Sydney, Australia's capital city. Just like in Wales, people were disappointed when Charles instead of Diana greeted them. In a letter to a friend in early April, while he and Diana were in Australia, he indicated his interest in her appeal. "Perhaps the wedding, because it was so well done and produced such a wonderful, almost Hollywood-style film, has distorted people's perceptions?"" he inquired.

Princess on the Rise

Diana was profoundly impacted by the public's enthusiastic support everywhere she went, along with the royal family's pained silence.

She learned that relating to people was her true gift and passion. She not only had a natural ability to relate with the public, but she also felt true empathy for them. Her desire to help those less fortunate had evolved from caring for cuddly animals as a child to caring for people all around the world. The reaction she received caused her to reconsider Charles. She was surprised by what she perceived to be his jealousy. That realization strengthened her and boosted her self-esteem. Maybe she was above it all. Diana couldn't help but feel good about her inherent ability to relate to others, despite being sick with bulimia and jet-lagged after crisscrossing the country. It wasn't just the fact that she was Charles' wife; it was her.

Diana confided in biographer Andrew Morton about her perception of Charles' envy of her. She remembered Charles blaming his poor performance in Australia on her. She tried to console him by claiming that no matter who his wife was, as Princess of Wales, she would be the center of attention. Diana told him she thought he should be proud of her only because she was his wife. However, she did not feel Charles regarded the issue in the same light.

Victor Chapman, the tour's press secretary, claimed he got multiple phone calls from Charles complaining about the lack of media coverage. The extraordinary news attention of Diana, Charles wrote to a friend, was likely to have a bad effect on her. After all, how could she possibly emerge with the same self-image? He was both correct and incorrect. Diana did, in fact, become obsessed with what the media was writing and saying about her. She devoured critiques of her performance in the tabloids and the more conventional British press when she returned from Australia. But was this a negative trend? Many would say that it just reinforced her self-esteem and gave her a greater sense of independence and self-worth.

A three-week trip to Canada later yielded the same results. While the media praised Diana, it mainly disregarded Charles. One Ottawa

Citizen piece even called him a "also-ran," which hurt him to the quick. "Why do they love her so much?" he questioned one of his friends. All she ever did was say 'yes' to me.`` It was at this point that Michael Colborne decided he'd had enough of getting caught up in their squabbles. Charles' long standing personal secretary, whom he had summoned to watch over Diana, quit in December after the prince accused him of spending too much time with her. Colborne, sensibly, responded that spending time with Diana was what he felt Charles wanted him to do, which enraged the prince. When Charles answered the door, Diana was sobbing as she listened to the onslaught. After a decade of service to Charles, Colborne decided to call it quits after the incident.

Diana, on the other hand, gained a sense of independence in how she reared William. She refused to implant in him what she saw as the pompous, self-indulgent attitude of a royal family member. She enrolled William (and later second son Harry) in Wetherby, a rather unpretentious Notting Hill preschool. Diana also did not instill in her sons an adoring and reverent attitude toward the royal family. A student once asked William if he knew Queen Elizabeth II when he was a child. "Aren't you talking about Granny?"" he inquired.11

Diana did not let her immense reputation and status as a princess overshadow her responsibilities as a mother. When the royal family refused to allow William to go on long official travels, like those to Australia and New Zealand, she retaliated by saying she would no longer go on such vacations. She didn't want to leave William in the hands of strangers while she traveled around the world. Diana, more than anyone, knew the anguish of children who do not have parents to support them emotionally. After all, she was harmed not only by her parents' divorce, but also by their lack of caring when she was a youngster. She had learned from her mistakes in the past and was not going to repeat them.

The same was true during her early years as Princess of Wales. She would demonstrate an independence of thought and action from this point forward, indicating her developing maturity. She was certainly upset when she discovered that Charles and Camilla were more than just friends, but instead of reacting like a weak and jealous schoolgirl, she used the strength and confidence she gained through success and maturity to become one of the world's most respected and admired women.

CHAPTER 8:
The Dying Marriage

Diana, the terrified, cringing, jealous woman, had vanished by the fall of 1983. Her doubts about Charles had turned into conviction, and she was confident he had renewed his romance with Camilla. But she defied her husband. She still wanted to save her marriage, but at some time she realized it was all over. She reached that stage on September 15, 1984, when she gave birth to her second son, Harry. Charles had freely expressed his preference for a girl, prompting Diana to keep the child's gender a secret from him. She reported that when Harry was born, Charles couldn't disguise his disappointment, even mocking the child's red hair, which was a Spencer attribute. "Something inside me died," Diana explained to friends at the time. It was the start of the end for the fairy tale pair.

And, while Charles had a penchant for strong women throughout his adult life, he wasn't impressed with his wife's sudden strength. One senior Buckingham Palace official described a marriage on the verge of dissolution as the mid-1980s approached, despite the fact that it officially lasted several years longer. "(Charles) didn't change his bachelor ways," claimed the official. "She desired that he remain at home with her and the children. It was the first time he'd been challenged, and she accepted. It was the first time he'd met someone on his level—he was surrounded by yes-men."

Despite Diana's denial that Charles was upset that she had given birth to another boy, her affection and concern for both William and Harry cannot be questioned. Even those who criticized Diana for her behavior during the marriage remarked on how much joy she gave to the union. The postpartum depression she had after the birth of William did not resurface after the birth of Harry. Her entire existence revolved around the guys. She planned parties for them and left messages on their doors professing her feelings for them. She was also a responsible mother, having them pick up their toys and limiting their sugar intake. Diana grew closer to William and Harry following her divorce, owing to her increased emotional demands, although she loved them from the time they were born.

Despite the fact that Diana and Charles were devoted to their children, they remained estranged. By the mid-1980s, it was clear that they had been mismatched from the outset. Diana had become the fashion darling of the United Kingdom. Every new clothing, hairstyle, and item of jewelry worn by the princess became media fodder. As images of the gorgeous Diana filled the front pages of the newspapers, Charles and the rest of the royal family were pushed to the inside pages. Diana's new haircut pushed Elizabeth II off the main page for the first time when she put her hair up for the first time during the 1984 State Opening of Parliament. New publications devoted primarily to the royal family centered nearly entirely on Diana and her children. Diana became increasingly conscious of the attention she was receiving for her wardrobe and began traveling with hundreds of various costumes.

While Charles was significantly more pensive and introspective, especially at that age, Diana was now in her mid-20s and more in tune with the entertainment industry. They attended the legendary Live Aid rock concert at Wembley Stadium in London in July 1985 to raise funds for starving Ethiopians. While Diana was seen dancing to the music of Madonna, David Bowie, and former Beatle Paul McCartney, Charles appeared bored and out of place in his coat and tie.

This game can be played by two people

Diana, persuaded that her husband had renewed his connection with Camilla, began flirting with her as well. Diana openly flirted with

An-drew Morton, a member of the press corps who later produced a disputed biography of the princess, according to reporter Judy Wade. The two had a continuing and amusing conversation about his colorful ties. Diana grabbed Morton's tie and drew him close to her during a cocktail reception, according to Wade, while stunned media members looked on. "God, I think I'll have to get a bucket of water and throw it over them," a press officer shouted. By the time Diana and Charles made their long-awaited vacation to America, the princess had established herself as the dominating figure in the relationship. Tina Brown, who went on to write a biography of Diana, wrote a story titled "The Mouse That Roared" in the October 1985 issue of Vanity Fair. It was highly negative to both. Brown alleged that the princess had complete control over Charles. She said that Diana's celebrity had harmed her and that Charles was irritable, uninteresting, and older than his 36 years. She went on to say that Diana was concerned with her public image and was addicted to shopping and reading about herself in the news.

The highlight of Diana's U.S. tour was a luncheon and ball hosted by President and Mrs. Reagan, during which she danced with American star John Travolta. Diana tried to spice up her relationship with Charles two months later by slipping into a slinky white satin gown and dancing seductively for him at an event at the Royal Opera House in Covent Garden. The dances went against the royal grain, but many in the audience were captivated by her stunning performance. Charles, however, was not one of them. He replied coolly to what he saw as an exhibition that went against royal protocol. He was clearly dissatisfied.

Was the marriage over by that point? Though Charles claimed that he spoke with Camilla only once during a five-year period—to announce Diana's first pregnancy—and that he returned to Camilla only after the marriage had irretrievably lost, many close to the couple believe Charles' physical relationship with Camilla began in

1983. Diana bemoaned that when William was born, the pair rarely slept in the same bed. Friends of Charles believe they engineered a reconciliation between him and Camilla in 1986 because he was unhappy and wanted someone to talk to. Charles had always thought Ca-milla was an excellent confidante. She, too, was in an unpleasant marriage at the time, which caused friends to intervene, particularly the same Patti Palmer-Tomkinson who had been won over by Diana before the wedding. Phone calls quickly developed into dates, and dates into sexual meetings. When Charles rekindled his connection with Camilla, he had no intention of doing so, according to Charles. But he was at a loss for words. "Frequently I feel nowadays that I'm in a kind of cage, pacing up and down in it, longing to be free," he wrote to a friend in late 1986. "How terrible incompatibility is, and how horribly destructive it can be." ...Though physical proof that Charles had resumed his affair with Camilla between the births of William and Harry has never existed, the hunting expeditions together and the time away from home indicate that his claim that they spoke only once by phone until 1986 was incorrect. Diana discovered Charles on the phone with Camilla on several occasions, which prompted suspicions. When Diana brought up her concerns about his connection with Camilla, he stayed silent. Diana felt betrayed after convincing herself that they were back together. Camilla became known as "the Rottweiler" because "she looks like a dog—and because once she gets her teeth into someone, she won't let go."

Many believe Diana refused to let go of Barry Mannakee, a personal protection officer with whom she had a strong relationship in the mid-1980s. Though she had come out of her shell by that point, she was still emotionally needy, especially since she believed Charles had resumed sexual relations with Camilla. Mannakee gave Diana the solace and praise she desperately needed. When she was upset and crying, she often fell into his arms. The friendship developed into a friendly and flirtatious one. She addressed him as "my fella" and sexily ran her hands over her evening gown before asking him, "Do I look all right?"" He'd respond, "I could quite fancy you myself," to which she'd murmur, "But you already do, don't you?""

Such discussions were sure to become viral. Mannakee was getting too near to Diana, according to senior protection officer Colin Trimming. Mannakee was fired in 1986 and sadly died the following year in a motorcycle accident. Diana suspected foul play, but she eventually discovered that a young motorist seeking her license had accidentally killed him. Mannakee was Diana's dearest friend, someone she could confide in. She saw him as a parent or an elder brother and insisted they never had sex, despite the fact that a decade later she told Charles's biographer Anthony Holden that Mannakee, who had a wife and two children, was the love of her life. Charles was aware of his wife's contact with Mannakee, but assumed it was nonsexual. Even if he had doubts, he insisted that they had nothing to do with his decision to resume his affair with Camilla.

There's a new girl in town

Camilla wasn't Diana's only adversary. Sarah Ferguson married Prince Andrew at Westminster Abbey in the summer of 1986, becoming the Duchess of York. She was a year older than Diana and more effervescent and worldly. She stepped into her post without a hitch, at least for the time being, and the royal family loved her right once. "Fergie" exhibited great spirit in spending time with the queen, the Queen Mother, and the Duke of Edinburgh on her first trip to Balmoral, a yearly holiday Diana hated. Mrs. Danvers of the High-grove staff could be overheard yelling her displeasure at the idea of another excursion to the castle she despised. Fergie, on the other hand, waxed lyrical about "the perfect haven, a stalwart fortress against the arrows." ..I enjoyed the crackling of its morning frost and the rich and earthy aromas of heather and peaty soil."

While Diana was still treated as an outsider by the royal family, Fergie fit right in. Charles not only noticed, but he was quick to point out the contrasts to his wife, asking her flatly why she couldn't be more like the Duchess of York. Fergie's presence did not make Diana feel frightened or angry. On the contrary, Fergie's involvement in the royal family provided her with someone her own age to relate to. Diana had known her for a long time. Fergie admired Diana and truly loved her company, despite the fact that she blended in with the royal family with far more desire and success. Diana, on the other hand, didn't mind Sarah taking over the media spotlight for a little period. Let her every step be scrutinized and re-examined, thought the Princess of Wales. And, to put it simply, she had more fun with Fergie than she had with anyone else since her carefree days at Coleherne Court. In a failed attempt to crash Andrew's bachelor celebration, the two dressed as police officers. They were arrested and thrown into a police van before being identified and released. They went to a local nightclub and drank champagne while becoming crazy. Diana had been looking forward to this kind of thoughtless pleasure since she married.

Fergie was also entertaining. She not only urged Diana to dance the can-can with her at a party she and Andrew gave to honor those who organized their wedding, but she also sought to entice the visitors to leap into the swimming pool fully clothed. In June 1987, she and Fergie were photographed with an um-brella poking a courtier on the behind. The stunt was universally condemned as juvenile, and some believed that it contributed to Charles' disdain for his wife. Diana, on the other hand, was simply having fun. As time passed, both she and Fergie mocked the stuffiness of royal family protocol.

However, Diana felt slighted by the royal family's attitude to Fergie, who, in Diana's opinion, was embraced with wide arms for who she was while Diana was overlooked for what she did. Fergie's ability to blend in with the royal family garnered her accolades and admiration. Diana's charisma and performance, which drew millions to her side all around the world, delivered nothing but stillness. The disparities in reactions widened the gap between Diana and the royal family. An already indifferent and frigid relationship became much colder. However, Diana's anguish at Fergie's acceptance by the royal family showed that she still cared about their feelings toward her.

She may not have lost her affections for Charles at the time, but she was certain that her husband was back with Camilla. That was the start of her romantic relationship with Major James Hewitt. Her beauty so captivated him that he planned to meet her at a party at the St. James Palace residence of lady-in-waiting Hazel West. He struck up a conversation with Diana about horseback riding, having been granted an invitation. As staff captain of the Household Division and commander of the Household Division stables, he was an experienced rider. She told him about her desire to overcome her phobias of horseback riding, which she'd had since falling off a horse as a child. She called him a few days later and scheduled lessons near Kensington Palace. Though Hewitt, an experienced instructor, claimed they both fully enjoyed the sessions, it has been argued that Diana was motivated more by her sexual attraction to Hewitt than by her desire to ride. They certainly spiced up her otherwise monotonous daily routine. Charles' rejection was as much sexual as anything else, and she was ready to deliver the same message back to him. Diana's affair was not her first, but it was her first open one.

Hewitt recounted one lesson that occurred after he was promoted to acting major and stationed in Windsor. He was overjoyed that Diana wanted to continue her lessons despite the additional travel. When she indicated she wanted to be alone with him, he quickly realized she had something else in mind. He remembers the first time he spent the night was at a dinner invitation. A full-fledged romantic relationship ensued, complete with love poems, hand holding, and secret rendezvous. Diana confessed in a 1995 magazine interview that she had instantly fallen in love with Hewitt, who felt the same way about her. They frequently told each other about their love, which made both of them feel desirable. It was just what Diana required on an emotional level. Given the rarity of her sexual experiences with Charles, she was somewhat inexperienced in bed prior to her romance with Hewitt. But, perilous as it was, he was charmed by their love life as they moved covertly from Kensington Palace to High-grove to his mother's home in Devon to avoid suspicion. "She was utterly charming, natural, fresh, vivacious, and rather lovely," Hewitt said. "There was an immediate chemistry. ...She was a woman who had been deeply wounded by rejection. Whether it was true or not, she regarded herself as being completely alone in a hostile world." Diana began opening up to him shortly before their first sexual encounter. She talked about being unloved by Charles, how the queen didn't appreciate her performance as Princess of Wales, how she wished her marriage to Charles had turned out differently, and how she believes the royal family is jealous of her popularity in comparison to her husband's. Diana's frailties became clear to Hewitt. She also admitted to him that she had bulimia, a subject she had avoided even with the slew of psychoanalysts she had visited. She said she didn't see it when she was with him, but he acknowledged being repulsed by it and noticing its consequences in her skin and loss of firmness. Hewitt, on the other hand, never saw her binge and purge in the time he spent with her, which was often up to two days at a time.

It was impossible to conceal such a friendship from everyone. The Royal Protection Squad officers were made aware of it, as was Queen Elizabeth II, who was briefed by Diana. The princess mustered the strength to tell her, convinced that she was the only one who could help. She complained about Charles's infidelity to the queen, who replied that it was not her duty to intervene. Diana later stated that the queen expressed powerlessness in the face of the crisis. "I don't know what you should do," said the queen. "Charles is completely hopeless."

Diana's self-esteem suffered as a result of her perceived hopelessness and lack of affection from Charles. Her time with Hewitt provided her with some of her few moments of happiness. Despite the fact that many of the media continued to believe in the fairy tale marriage, which had been rubbish since the honeymoon, it was clear by 1987 that the relationship was in shambles. During a June wedding ceremony, Diana danced seductively with handsome banker Philip Dunne, while Charles spent much of the night with old girlfriend Anna Wallace before lovingly dancing with Camilla. At 2:00 a.m., he eventually requested Diana to go, but she allegedly laughed in his face and proceeded to party. She was in her late twenties, sexually fulfilled for the first time in her life, and blossoming into a social butterfly.

Though friends and relatives might identify a problem in the marriage or were aware of relationships involving Charles or Diana, the media had a more difficult time detecting it because their public relationship remained effective. In fact, during an official visit to Australia to commemorate its bicentennial in 1988, they pretended to be loving spouses for the cameras. Diana agreed to go along for the ride as Princess of Wales, and Charles maintained the public perception of a happy spouse, all of which allowed the marriage to survive, at least legally, for a long period. But the tide had long changed in favor of a marriage of convenience and eventual divorce. They spent much of their time apart, only meeting up for official events.

Diana and Hewitt love affair, on the other hand, was doomed to fail. In the end, she had to admit that "his head was inside his trousers" and that "he was about as interesting as a knitting pattern."10 Critics of their relationship believed that they were manipulating each other and that neither was ever truly in love, though both have attempted to dispel that notion. Some saw Hewitt as the appropriate man at the right moment for Diana's sexual and emotional needs, while Diana gave Hewitt the red carpet treatment. Hewitt paid frequent visits to Diana and became close to William and Harry, telling them bedtime tales and playing with them at Highgrove.

Butler Paul Burrell frequently felt caught in the crossfire of Diana and Charles's love lives. Burrell recounted Diana's covert request to pick up Hewitt and drive him to meet her, after which the two fell into a passionate hug. However, he stated that his dealings with Charles's friendship with Camilla occurred before Diana and Hewitt. "It should be noted that Major James Hewitt visited Highgrove long after Camilla Parker Bowles," Burrell wrote. "Prince Charles was the first to strike in this direction. The princess simply surpassed her husband's level of deception."

However, the shallowness of that relationship was eventually revealed. Diana didn't think Hewitt was particularly bright. She was developing intellectually and becoming more aware of her surroundings. Some had begun to regard her as a party girl, with socializing taking precedence over her sons. However, by the late 1980s, the woman who had shown such empathy for others less fortunate as a kid and teenager was displaying those traits once more. Her life was characterized by her deep concern for others till its untimely conclusion.

CHAPTER 9:
Increasing Compassion

The 1980s were the decade of the Great Divide in both the United Kingdom and the United States. The divide between affluent and poor has expanded significantly. And, despite the fact that Diana came from nobility and now lived as royalty, both of which clearly benefited from policies that favored the wealthy, the misery of those who suffered drew out her inherent compassion. The difference now was that she had the celebrity and influence to make a difference. When it came to raising contributions, her sheer presence at a philanthropic event was enough to set the ball going.

Diana didn't have to modify herself to make a difference in the world. Her growing commitment in social concerns, in fact, allowed her to temporarily forget about her personal troubles. However, a reunion with an old friend, Carolyn Bartholomew, forced her to confront her bulimia in the spring of 1988. Bartholomew, who cared enough for Diana to be unhappy with her for letting the condition linger for so long, threatened to alert the media of her illness if she didn't take quick steps to cure herself. Diana was taken aback by the confrontation. She realized she had to act, not only because of the threat of reporters splashing the news all over the front pages of newspapers around the world, but also because the words of one of her best friends brought her back to reality.

Diana's next action was to telephone Dr. Maurice Lipsedge, an eating disorder specialist at Guy's Hospital in Central London who had previously worked with her sister Sarah in the late 1970s. Diana was taken aback when he asked how many times she had attempted suicide, and she replied four or five times. Lipsedge continued to ask her pointed questions before declaring that if she could keep her meals down, he could treat her in six months. He also suggested that she study books on her condition to better understand it and that the source of her problem was her husband. The medicines' instant success has been questioned. According to biographer Andrew Morton, despite Charles's sarcastic remarks and lack of confidence in the treatments, Diana's bouts with bulimia decreased from four or five times a week to once every three weeks, but they increased dramatically whenever she stayed with the royal family at Balmoral, Sandringham, or Windsor.1 They also worsened when she spent significant time with Charles at Highgrove, which she claimed to Mor-ton she still despises.

In any case, her struggle to conquer bulimia coincided with her resolve to confront Camilla Parker Bowles, the lady of her nightmares. It happened the night she and Charles went to Camilla's sister Annabel Elliott's 40th birthday party. Because Diana and Charles had spent so little time together, the guests assumed she wouldn't turn up. And she might not have if she hadn't come with a certain goal in mind. Diana discovered Camilla downstairs with Charles and a few other guests. She invited everyone save Camilla to go upstairs, claiming that she needed to speak with her. Though she was terrified when she heard a disturbance upstairs from those who had accurately predicted a fight, Diana told Camilla that she was aware of her romance with Charles and that she believed Camilla and the prince were treating her like an ignorant "idiot."

Diana further said that Charles yelled at her in the car on the way home, to which she responded with a long weeping fit. She didn't get much sleep that night, but the next morning she felt as if a big weight had been lifted off her shoulders. Though she claimed to her husband that she simply told Camilla that she still loved him and wanted to be a good wife and mother, her actions following the confrontation with his mistress indicate that she was ready to let go of the pettiness and jealousy that had kept her from reaching her full potential. She unquestionably did not choose fidelity over a continuing sexual relationship with Hewitt and, eventually, other men at that time.

The connection with Hewitt was obviously not meant to last. They were not just intellectually dissimilar, but he was assigned to lead a tank unit in Germany for two years in late 1989. The United Kingdom was on high alert owing to East German rebellions, which some feared would lead to Soviet Union military action. Diana was dissatisfied and wanted to work out a plan that would allow them to meet at least once a week. When Hewitt declined, citing his feeling of responsibility, she was enraged. Hewitt couldn't be faulted. Events in East Germany were having a major impact not only on that country, but also on Europe and the rest of the world. East Germans tired of Communist and totalitarian rule tore down the Berlin Wall, forcing their leaders to reconcile with West Germany after nearly a half-century estrangement.

The Missions of the Heart

Though Diana appeared to be considerably more interested in her personal life than in the status of the globe, the same could not be said of her sympathy for those in need. In early 1989, she embarked on her first solo tour in the United States. Diana requested to spend the most of her time in New York City, but not for the nightlife. Rather, she requested visits to the city's poorest, most drug-infested ghettos and the crumbling Harlem Hospital, where she met eight AIDS-infected newborns who would most certainly die before reaching their first birthday.

Diana also made friends with officials at Henry Street, a social welfare organization that worked with battered women and the homeless and had grown to be one of the best in the country. Henry Street had a high reputation for hiring the homeless and poor. But Henry Street needed money to continue its operations. It has been threatened with a financial cut. Although officials had had terrible encounters with celebrities, some of whom were simply looking for attention by donating their names to such a philanthropic endeavor, they soon learned that Diana's compassion and willingness to help were genuine. "She was genuinely concerned about the issues," said Verona Middleton-Jeter, former director of the Urban Family Center. "She had many inquiries about. ..what the battered women were experiencing. ...I just wasn't expecting such truthfulness. She wasn't a princess or a member of royalty. ...She had an easy rapport with the residents. It felt organic and welcoming."

Diana had always been selfless and concerned about people who were less fortunate. Not only did these characteristics become more pronounced over time, but she also learned a lot more about matters about which she was passionate. Rather than using her fame and fortune to create a beautiful life for herself, she used it to serve others. She felt instinctively as a teenager that she had a life goal, and she initially thought it revolved around a future marriage. However, in her capacity as princess, she recognized it was far more poignantly tied to delivering kindness to people who had been treated unkindly, help to the helpless, and hope to the hopeless. Furthermore, she possessed a natural ability to express her emotions to those same people, as well as those who cared about them.

Marjatta van Boeschoten, a former lawyer and trustee for Paradise House Association, a learning institution for disadvantaged individuals, was among those who observed Diana's enchantment. When van Boeschoten realized Diana was coming to visit in 1983, she felt little excitement or delight. She was taken aback when she saw Diana with one of her staff members. "There was a radiance and warmth about her, as well as her beauty," van Boeschoten recalled. "Her vulnerability was palpable. I watched how she leaned forward and listened intently to one of the caretakers, giving her undivided attention. It still moved the caregiver a year later. It was as if light had reached everyone there that morning."

Such a story would not have surprised Patrick Jephson, who joined Diana's entourage as an equerry before becoming her private secretary in 1988. Jephson was stunned by a scene Diana had with a dying kid on his first day working with her. He quickly recognized Diana was deeply moved by the incident and felt genuine sympathy for the youngster's circumstances. That startled him because he had been taken aback by her crude humor in more private occasions, sometimes at the cost of the individuals she was seeing. But Jephson quickly learned that laughing about difficult and painful activities was her emotional coping mechanism. As soon as he saw the time she spent with the dying child, he knew she was completely sincere. Her reaction when the girl died added validity to the story.

"As I watched her at a dying child's bedside, holding the girl's newly cold hand and comforting the stricken parents, she seemed to share their grief," Jephson said in his Diana biography. "Not self-consciously as a stranger, distantly as a counselor, or even through any special experience or deep insight." Instead, it appeared that a sense of calm had gathered about her. The crying mother and heartbroken father poured their grief into this silence, and it felt safe there. The young woman in the nice suit and soulful eyes had no answers for them, but they had the impression that she understood at least some of what they were feeling. That was all that was required at the time."

No epidemic touched Diana's heart more than AIDS, which was first diagnosed in 1983 and became one of the decade's deadliest diseases. It not only caused patients to die slowly, but it also frequently made them social outcasts. Though anyone can be infected with the HIV virus that causes AIDS, the outbreak had a significant impact on the homosexual community. Diana had a lot of LGBT friends in the fashion industry and on the royal staff. Stephen Barry, Charles' valet, was among those who died from AIDS. She felt safe and unburdened with homosexual guys, and she was in a lot of anguish as the sickness spread and threatened her friends.

Ignorance regarding HIV has always been pervasive, but it was especially prevalent in the 1980s, when the disease was still relatively new. Many people were reluctant to approach someone who had been positively diagnosed. As a result, when Diana was invited to the opening of the first AIDS unit in England at Middlesex Hospital, there was much conjecture about how she would manage the issue. Many others appeared to lose their trepidation when she shook hands with 12 AIDS sufferers without gloves. "You could almost feel the taboos being broken," claimed Daily Mail photographer Richard Kay. "I consider myself to be a reasonably liberal, open-minded person, but I was quite surprised."

Professionals like professor Michael Adler, who was working with AIDS patients at the time, were also affected. Adler, who later became the British government's senior adviser on sexual health issues, was caught aback by Diana's gesture, especially given the widespread belief that the disease was only of a sexual nature that affected gay males. Diana, according to Adler, brought a touch of compassion to the subject, dispelling falsehoods in the process. Diana suddenly hugged a seven-year-old kid who had been diagnosed with HIV during a trip to New York two years later. "Previously, people didn't like the overall ambiance," Adler explained. "It was observed to be primarily occurring among gay men, and it involved sex, all of which we are not adept at dealing with, but she actually cut through that." She gave it credibility and a face."

Some have argued, or even claimed, that Diana's sensitive moments with the sick, dying, or impoverished were far from genuine. She had always desired to be loved—not only by a member of the opposing sex, but by the general public. The psychological trauma she had as a youngster, first when she correctly perceived her parents' sadness that she was born a female, then when they separated and divorced, left her yearning to be loved. She desired not only true romantic love from Charles and other men in her life, but also respect and admiration from people all over the world. Critics who refer to Diana's philanthropic appearances argue that she was on her own personal stage, that she was the same girl who raised her arms on the diving board as a toddler and said, "Look at me, look at me!"" They believe that her performances became mechanical, almost robotic as she smiled for the cameras, and that her compassion for others became a show for the media as well as a cure for what ailed her emotionally."

However, expressing such an attitude to a father of a sick child, an administrator from a hospital's AIDS ward, or a nameless, faceless poor African boy seen by Diana might elicit an indignant response. They were all convinced that she genuinely cared. Many of them had seen false performances before, and what better way to draw attention to a cause than to put on a show in front of a camera and send a photograph around the world?

"Look, it doesn't really matter to me why she wanted to do this kind of thing," Margaret Jay of the National Aids Trust of the United Kingdom stated, her voice tinged with rage. "We live in a world where celebrities wield enormous influence to assist groups like mine. This one chose to, for which I am grateful. That's the end of the story."

Still Looking for Love

Diana couldn't be blamed for wanting to fill an emotional emptiness. By 1989, her connection with Hewitt had faded into obscurity. And butler Paul Burrell was noticing that on many nights, the odometer on Prince Charles' vintage Aston Martin would read 22 miles—exactly the duration of a round trip to Camilla Parker Bowles' Middlewich House. Burrell frequently got communication indicating that Charles would be spending the night at a different location on specific occasions. Terrible conflicts broke out on the rare times that Diana and Charles were together. Burrell reported hearing heated voices, slamming doors, and then silence. The battles became violent at times. On a Sunday night, he entered the sitting room, where he had laid a table for two, only to find broken glass and spilt water, as well as Prince Charles on his hands and knees, cleaning up cutlery. Diana was nowhere to be found.

Diana was haunted by her husband's lack of love, and despite their sexual experiences with others, she tried to win him over. Diana's psychological trauma from her unfulfilling relationship with Charles drove her to seek peace and tranquility from dubious sources such as astrologers, masseurs, and even tarot card readers. In an attempt to attain inner calm, she tried aromatherapy, hypnotherapy, and acupuncture. Despite overwhelming evidence to the contrary, Diana clung to her marriage in the summer of 1989. Her relatives and the royal family both put pressure on her to work on rebuilding her connection with Charles. She even agreed to have another child, but the marriage had been irreparably damaged. Any attempt to settle their issues led to additional squabbles, threats, and accusations. Diana started to be associated with old acquaintance James Gilbey, whom she met when she was 17 and who had become wealthy by dealing in costly used vehicles, in the fall of 1989, about the time Hewitt left for Germany. Their friendship began with largely lamenting about failed love lives, but it quickly blossomed into a romance. Gilbey spoke affectionately to Diana, even giving her the nickname "Squidgy." Their growing feelings were strongly suggested by a taped phone conversation on New Year's Eve that year, in which both spoke of their feelings for each other, though it became clear that he was far more taken with her than she was with him. The tape soon made its way into the hands of enthusiastic media members, who called it "Squidgygate." It wasn't the only such tape in circulation. Camilla and Charles had a passionate and sexually graphic phone discussion that year, during which Charles declared he wanted to be a tampon. "Camillagate" was created.

Diana's relationship with Gilbey was flourishing in late 1989, but she still had feelings for Hewitt. Even the New Year's Eve talk proved that Gil-bey was considerably more devoted to her than she was to him. She expressed her gratitude to Gilbey, but he addressed her as "darling" throughout the chat, a gesture of love she did not return. In reality, if Squidgygate proved anything, it was that Diana saw Gilbey as little more than a trusted friend, despite the fact that she was overheard kissing him on the phone. Furthermore, the likelihood that she had a sexual relationship with Gilbey to replace the one she had with Hewitt cannot be ruled out. The topic soon shifted to her relationship with the royal family, which was exacerbated by another stressful holiday season. Diana claimed that she had been overcome by grief, that she felt constrained by the constraints of her marriage, and that Charles had made her life a "real torture."

In late June 1990, a week after William's eighth birthday, an event occurred that signaled the end of any attempt at reconciliation. When Charles fell off his polo pony, he shattered his right arm. He was eventually told that his arm wasn't mending properly, and he was brought to Nottingham's Queen's Medical Centre for surgery. Diana jumped at the chance to pick him up from the hospital and bring him home, where she could express her concern while nursing him back to health. But when she tried to mother him, he rejected her and told her he wanted to be alone. Camilla arrived at Highgrove to be by his side as she drove back to London in tears. Burrell remembered Charles' delight at seeing her. Burrell stated that the royal wedding was officially doomed from that point forward. By August, the world's attention had shifted to the Middle East. Following Iraq's invasion and ruthless annexation of Kuwait, the United Kingdom and scores of other countries joined an American-led troop surge in Saudi Arabia, as well as in the Persian Gulf and Red Sea. Diana had resumed her affair with Hewitt, who had returned home from Germany, just before Christmas. However, when Operation Desert Storm began in January, he was transported to the Persian Gulf. Diana mailed him up to four impassioned letters a day, expressing her yearning for him and her deep dissatisfaction with her dishonest marriage. She also expressed her dissatisfaction that the relationship between Charles and Camilla had not been covered by the media, a fact that grew on her over time.

During the Gulf War, Diana's sentiments for Hewitt were disclosed by his estranged girlfriend Emma Stewardson, who claimed to the News of the World that the princess had been sending gifts and love letters to the major. Diana was terrified by the media claims, notwithstanding Stewardson's denial of a sexual relationship between the two. After all, it was her husband's infidelity, not her own, that she wanted made public. Hewitt paid Diana a visit when he returned from the war. He felt compelled to hide in the trunk of the car en route to see her since press scrutiny had grown so severe. Things would become far less comfortable. To avoid further suspicion, Diana distanced herself from Hewitt, who felt rejected as a result. Rather than calling him or meeting him in private to say goodbye, she just stopped answering his calls.

Although the Gulf War had been won, the war between Diana and Charles was still ongoing. Both were informed on June 3, 1991, that their son Wil-liam had been injured in the head with a golf club at his boarding school. They rushed to Royal Berkshire Hospital, where they were relieved to see William sitting up and awake in his bed. His doctor explained his injury to them as a depressed fracture in the forehead. For surgery, William was sent to Great Ormond Street

Hospital. When Diana and Charles were told that the operation would be safe, Charles chose to keep his evening and morning appointments before returning to visit William after the surgery. In the media, all hell broke loose. Charles was criticized by the Daily Mirror and the Sun for departing while his wife remained by William's side. Diana later complained to reporters that her husband had accused her of misrepresenting the seriousness of their son's condition, making him appear insensitive. Diana was appalled by both the tragedy and the prince's alleged lack of concern, according to Gilbey. She even told a friend, Adrian Ward-Jackson, "I can't be with someone who behaves like that." The media frequently praised Diana's affections for her two sons while downplaying Charles', despite the fact that both were devoted parents. Photographers captured William throwing himself into his mother's embrace after the couple returned from an official visit to Canada. More photos of Charles waving his arms in greeting to the boys were captured seconds later. Despite this, the British media solely published photographs of Diana giddily ready to hug her children. Diana's photograph was, in fact, one of the most famous of her married life.

A Doomed Relationship

Aside from their official roles, Diana was rarely seen with Charles once all emotional ties had been severed. That realization hit butler Paul Burrell when he accompanied the couple to Japan in November 1990. He considered them as little more than business associates who were only together because of their work obligations. They even remained in different rooms. Burrell had no connection with Diana and was surprised by her sudden temper and touchiness over little matters. It was the first time he had felt uneasy in her company. Not only did she no longer have love for Charles, but she had also become tired of the rigid scheduling and etiquette that came with being the Princess of Wales.

Meanwhile, Burrell observed Diana's humiliation as Charles continually criticized her appearance and performance. Charles may have taken every opportunity to attack Diana's fashion sense because she was well known for being fashion-conscious. Diana dressed in all black and white for an afternoon event during an official visit to Czechoslovakia in May 1991, when they stayed not only in separate apartments but on separate floors of President Havel's opulent Prague mansion. In front of Diana and all the officials present, Charles remarked, "You look like you've just joined the Mafia."11 If his objective was to elicit laughter, he failed entirely. If his goal was to humiliate his wife, he was successful.

By this point, it was hard to look at the royal marriage through rose-colored glasses, even though most casual observers, as well as those who extensively examined the relationship, believed divorce was unimaginable. However, Diana's new financial adviser, Joseph Sanders, and old friend and adviser Dr. James Colthurst began preparing her for a split from Charles that would still present her in a favorable light. A possible outlet for such a scenario would be a biography of Diana written by freelance writer Andrew Morton, who had previously covered the royal family in the press. Colthurst was well acquainted with Morton, and the two frequently battled in squash matches. He scheduled a brunch meeting with Morton, during which they discussed Diana's sorrow, which revolved around her failed marriage, bulimia, and other mental and emotional problems. They discussed Diana's dissatisfaction with the royal family's treatment of her, as well as the affair between Charles and Camilla Parker Bowles, which Diana saw as the end of their relationship. In a country obsessed with royal family news and a world that admired Diana, discoveries like Charles' infidelity and Diana's unsuccessful suicide attempts had to make the book a huge hit.

All Morton needed were Diana's ideas. Colthurst informed the princess about the biography intentions, but she hesitated. Rather than merely thinking things out, she decided to look to the sky for guidance. Colthurst enlisted the help of friend Felix Lyle to conduct an astrological reading for Diana. Though Diana had her own astrologers, Lyle would provide an objective astrological perspective, if such a thing exists. They discussed Neptune's deception and Pluto's strength in her chart before Lyle and the princess revealed that the planets and stars had aligned favorably. The biography was a success.

Morton never interviewed Diana, who insisted on remaining blameless in the event of a backlash. She might disclaim any involvement with the book, absolving Morton of any culpability. She wanted the chance to inform Charles and other members of the royal family that the book had been written without her permission. Diana and Colthurst then made tape recordings, which were provided to Morton, who then asked the princess further questions. She agreed to let him interview her friends. Though Hewitt declined the opportunity to talk with Morton, others such as Gilbey and Bartholomew jumped at the chance.

The world was about to learn what Diana and Charles had suspected since their honeymoon more than a decade before: their marriage had failed. They were going to find out why, much to the joy of those who idolized the princess or devoured every delicious nugget of knowledge about the royal family.

CHAPTER 10:
Their Separation

While Morton was busy writing a biography that would reveal, among other things, Charles and Camilla's love affair, images published by the Daily Mail revealed that Diana's marriage wasn't the only royal marriage in jeopardy. Sarah, Duchess of York, was photographed with Texas multimillionaire Steve Wyatt, son of Saks Fifth Avenue heiress Lynn Sakowitz Wyatt. In mid-March 1990, Sarah and Andrew announced their divorce.

However, by the time those images were published, Sarah had already begun a relationship with another affluent Texan, John Bryan. An Italian photographer followed the pair to a remote vacation site and took over 200 photos of them kissing, including one in which Bryan kissed the tops of her feet. The Mirror bought over 50 of the photographs, one of which became renowned as the "toe-sucking picture."

Despite their differences since the latter joined the royal family, Diana and Sarah appeared to be moving in the same path. In fact, it was thought that Sarah was pressuring Diana to divorce her husband, just as she had divorced Andrew. Diana and Charles' marriage appeared to be on the rocks during a February 1992 vacation of India, when he did not accompany her to the iconic Taj Mahal. Photographers crowded to Diana, completely ignoring Charles, who was speaking at a business meeting. Though photos of Diana standing alone in front of a symbol of love like the Taj Mahal, built by a Mogul emperor for his bride, could be melancholy and a testament to a failing marriage, she didn't appear to mind.

In fact, she seemed to enjoy the idea that her fairy tale marriage had come crashing down.

Photographer Jayne Fincher inquired about Diana's feelings on the Taj Mahal, to which she responded in a cryptic manner, mentioning the monument's healing properties. Members of the media instantly picked up on the message that she needed such a thoughtful moment at the Taj Mahal to get her mind off her husband's treatment. Diana, who was expected to give trophies to the winning team at a polo event two days later, issued a considerably more blatant repudiation of her husband. Diana approached a staff member and expressed her apprehension about kissing Charles in public. When Charles scored a goal, he approached Diana. Twas the night before Valentine's Day, and everyone was expecting a big smooch. Diana, on the other hand, turned her head and got pecked on the neck. The following day, publications all across the world stated that the poor kiss foreshadowed an even worse marriage.

Diana's father, Johnnie Spencer, died abruptly of a heart attack at Humana Hospital Wellington in north London the next month. Given that he had only been suffering from moderate pneumonia, the tragedy was rather startling. Diana and William had paid him a visit just four days before. She intended to go home alone from a family skiing trip, but Charles and his team tried to persuade her to fly with him for the sake of public impression. Diana had to be persuaded to give in by the queen. Despite his pleas for him and Diana to follow each other, Charles hurried to Highgrove upon arriving, leaving her to mourn over her father alone. On April 1, the prince arrived by helicopter for the funeral, then returned to London rather than attend the cremation. However, it was during the funeral that one magnificent, silent gesture put an end to her dispute with Raine, who was understandably heartbroken by her husband's unexpected death. Diana was sitting pretty far away from Rain during the ceremony, but she rose from her seat, approached her stepmother, took her hand in hers, and walked around the chapel with her. Frances Shand Kydd, on the other hand, went unnoticed at the funeral.

Meanwhile, Diana began to feel uneasy as the release of her biography approached. She had eagerly awaited its arrival at first, as her ambition to expose Charles and Camilla's love affair was about to be realized. However, a month before its release, she became concerned about the prospect of a bad reaction not only from the media and the general public, but also from family and friends. She even confessed her anxiety to film producer David Puttnam during a March dinner party when she discussed the dangers of AIDS. She began by telling him about her marriage's failures, then told him that she had written a book that she hoped would clear the air but would instead cause serious problems. "Now I think it was a very stupid thing to do that will cause all kinds of terrible trouble," Diana told Puttnam. "I'd like to rewind the film." It's the stupidest thing I've ever done."

The Tell-All Story

The world would soon find out how stupid it was. The Sunday Times announced that it would begin serializing the book on June 7. Andrew Neil, a newspaper editor, couldn't believe his eyes when he started reading portions from Morton's book. The revelations stunned him. He was suspicious about its veracity until Morton looked over the book's sources with him and told him that there were many more. The Sunday Times took a risk by publishing such a strong condemnation of Prince Charles and the royal family, yet the paper nonetheless paid the British equivalent of $440,000 for the rights to print it. The newspaper put up billboards and broadcast television commercials announcing the book's serialization. Rival publications attempted to cast doubt on the book's validity by alleging it lacked royal authorization, but their efforts were futile.

The first section discussed Diana's bulimia, her half-hearted suicide attempts, and, of course, Charles and Camilla's romance. Diana spun in both directions as a result of her overwhelming dread. According to Daily Mirror editor Richard Stott, she assured photographer Kent Gavin that she had not collaborated in any way with the book's authorship, a claim that the newspaper went with in a screaming page-one headline on June 8. Morton quickly fulfilled his end of the bargain with Diana by accepting full responsibility for the contents of the book, which undermined his efforts. After all, how believable would a biography of Diana be without Diana's input?

Lord McGregor, Chairman of the Press Complaints Commission, set out to find out. He called Diana's brother-in-law, Robert Fellowes, the queen's private secretary for 15 years. Diana stated again, this time to Fellowes, that she had nothing to do with the book. Fellowes and the queen's press secretary, Charles Anson, relayed Morton's denial to McGregor, who then issued a statement claiming that all press coverage of the royal marriage had been a "odious exhibition of journalists dabbling their fingers in the stuff of other people's souls." However, when sections from the book began to publish, it became clear that Diana had made significant contributions to its substance. The media were informed of her impending visit to Bartholomew, who had been quoted in the book on the issue of the princess's bulimia. There could no longer be any dispute once images of the two chatting were published in British media. McGregor, Fellowes, and others who felt duped by Diana were enraged when she denied her involvement in Morton's biography. Diana was awed by the possibility of accompanying the royal family on all of the yearly summer celebrations after learning about her involvement in the book.

Members of the British press slammed Morton and his accomplices, claiming that their work was mostly made up. They slammed the Sunday Times for publishing the portions. Their outrage was fueled by many British journalists' belief that the royal family is sacred. According to one writer, Morton was more concerned with money than with the royal family's safety. Others were still skeptical that Diana had contributed to the book's substance.

The princess was concerned about public reaction, but that concern was alleviated during a June 12 visit to a Merseyside hospice, her first formal engagement since the extracts were published. A crowd of thousands cheered her as she appeared in front of a waiting audience. Diana began to scream hysterically after an elderly woman stroked her face. The tears flowed not only from the gesture and a sense of oneness with the people, but also from the years of anguish she had endured. It was a release of feelings she had been holding in.

After reading the newspaper excerpts, Charles experienced some emotions as well. He had hoped against hope that such damning phrases had come from Diana's acquaintances rather than his wife. After the kiss-on-the-neck event in India, Charles had already discussed a possible separation with the queen, but he was told to grin and bear it for another six months. However, the findings in Morton's book put an end to that notion. The infidelity of a prince is far from disgraceful, based on historical traditions and the urgings of such valued friends as Lord Mountbatten; the idea of criticizing and sharing secrets about the royal family was thought unforgivable.

On June 15, the day before the book was to be published, a hastily planned meeting with the queen and the Duke of Edinburgh was organized at Windsor Castle. Despite the fact that Diana's involvement in the book could scarcely be contested, she reaffirmed her claim. However, there was no going back at that moment. She refused to accept responsibility for whatever she had done. She expressed her loathing for Camilla and requested a trial separation from her powerful in-laws. The response was sharp and direct. The queen and Prince Philip urged that their disputes be resolved via compromise and altruistic approaches to their marriage for the benefit of their children, the royal family, and the country. Diana subsequently said that the confrontation was a welcome relief. For years, she couldn't have the bravery to voice her feelings to the royal family regarding Charles, Camilla, and her relationship with the royal family. Diana felt more at ease now that everything was out in the open.

The queen planned to further discuss the situation. She organized another meeting for the next day, but Diana declined to attend. She did, however, correspond frequently with Prince Philip, who acted as a mediator. In fact, the duke seemed more determined to save the marriage than his son. But Diana was irritated by the tone of her father-in-law's texts, in which he pushed her to reconsider how she had done in her marriage. While Diana should be commended for her charity work and solo tours, being the wife of Prince Charles "involved much more than simply being a hero with the British people." Diana was offended by the correspondences, especially since she had grown to respect Prince Philip over the years. The Duke of Edinburgh was just getting started. He went on to say that jealousy had afflicted the marriage, which Diana misinterpreted as a dig at her. But how does a woman keep from getting envious while her husband is having an affair with someone else? Diana was taken aback when he wrote that her husband had made "a considerable sacrifice" when he cut off his relationship with Camilla initially, and then asked her, "Can you honestly look into your heart and say that Charles' relationship with Camilla had nothing to do with your behavior towards him in your marriage?"”

However, by the summer, the open communication had changed their perspectives on one another. Diana's responses to Prince Philip's remarks strengthened his admiration for her. His notes began to sound nicer. She felt vindicated when a member of the royal family acknowledged that her rage was justified and not the result of a raving crazy. She appreciated the endeavor to understand her and even entertained the possibility that her marriage to Charles could be resurrected eventually. But she thought the separation was necessary at the time.

Any notion of a stable marriage connection seemed naive, especially when Morton's blockbuster bestseller hit the shelves and the media circus ensued. The Sunday Times tried in vain to elicit a statement from Charles about the book, but it did carry a piece on June 28 quoting his associates as stating the prince was irritated that Diana still refused complete collaboration with Morton. They went on to say that Charles only wanted Diana to recognize her role and apologize. Later that summer, the Squidgygate tapes were released, and an article in the Sun stated unequivocally that Diana had a physical relationship with James Hewitt. She filed a lawsuit against the newspaper, but she never went to court. Diana's humiliation over Charles's connection with Camilla was put into doubt now that the media had disclosed her suspected infidelity with both Gilbey and Hewitt. Friends said she was deeply upset by the harsh press.

The Last Legs of a Royal Wedding

The Prince and Princess of Wales arrived at their official engagements that autumn with an unmistakable coldness toward each other. Both had visited with lawyers about a prospective divorce or separation, and friends on both sides agreed that their personal interactions with each other frequently resulted in heated voices and upset sentiments. Diana initially refused to accompany Charles on an official trip to Korea, but the queen persuaded her to reconsider. The princess came, but she made little attempt to hide her lack of enthusiasm. Charles's depressed mood contributed to an overall picture that inspired tabloids to dub them "The Glums."[6] Charles wrote to a friend about his agony and his bleak perspective for the future.

Soon after, another in the seemingly endless published reports about the royal family's indiscretions hit the newsstands when the Daily Mirror and Sun ran excerpts of the sexually charged conversation between Charles and Camilla that quickly became known as "Camillagate." The lurid dialogue not only confirmed the prince's infidelity, but also called into question his suitability to be king of England.

As if public opinion of the monarchy hadn't already plummeted, a fire that raged through Windsor Castle on November 24 added fuel to the fire. Most British residents were outraged by the royal marriage's demise due to infidelity and backstabbing, but when it was suggested that they pay for the devastation through increased taxes, hostility erupted. Already a contentious question was whether or not the queen should pay any taxes at all. The damage inflicted by the flames is believed to be between $40 and $80 million. The citizens were perplexed as to why their financial obligations should be enhanced when the woman who represented the royal family was exempt from paying a shilling.

Meanwhile, neither Charles nor Diana were in the mood for compromise when they fought about who would accompany William and Harry on the weekend of November 19. The royal family assumed the boys would attend their father's shooting party, but Diana had planned to spend time with them alone because she couldn't face spending a weekend with her husband. And she didn't want to be surrounded by his pals during such a sensitive time. The flap proved to be the last straw. Charles had agonized over the potential of a legal separation, owing in large part to his family's determination that affairs with Diana be settled, but his rage won out. On November 25, Charles informed Diana of his choice at Kensington Palace. According to newspaper stories, the princess consented to separate straight away and appeared to be extremely satisfied, if not downright delighted, that evening. During a phone call that night, however, James Hewitt noticed a very different tone from Diana. "Diana sounded flat and low," observed Hewitt. "She didn't think she'd ever be able to have what she really wanted." What did Diana want? She had often told friends how much she envied them. She informed them that all she had ever wanted was to be truly loved, even if it meant living a life considerably simpler than the one she had been accustomed to as princess. Even after a four-year divorce, a modest existence was no longer an option. Diana would go down in history as one of the most well-known and revered ladies on the planet. She would seek unquestionable, unending affection for the remainder of her tragically short life.

While Diana pursued happiness and fulfillment, British Prime Minister John Major made a prepared message to parliamentarians. "It is announced from Buckingham Palace that, with regret, the Prince and Princess of Wales have decided to separate," Major stated. "Their Royal Highnesses have no intention of divorcing, and their constitutional positions will remain unaffected." This decision was reached peacefully, and they will both continue to actively engage in their children's upbringing. ...Their Royal Highnesses will continue to carry out full and separate public engagement schedules, as well as attend family and national events together on occasion."

Major then elicited a collective gasp when he said that divorce was out of the question and that Charles and Diana were still in line to be king and queen of England, respectively. Most people thought it was ridiculous that a couple who lived apart and took every chance as individuals to verbally trash their marriage should be considered heirs to the kingdom, especially at that time. The archbishop of Canterbury, who would eventually crown the couple, proposed two conditions: that both retain strong relationships with their sons and that all love encounters be kept private. The first would be simple. The second would not be attempted at all.

Following the split announcement, lawyers on both sides worked tirelessly to get the best possible agreement for their clients. Diana didn't object when it was made clear that all solo excursions she made as Princess of Wales would not be made as an official representative of the queen. Diana was in the daily care of William and Harry due to the split custody arrangement. She obtained residency in a magnificent Kensington Palace apartment after a dispute over living arrangements. She wouldn't have to go to Highgrove on a weekly basis, which brought back so many bad memories for her. Diana was obviously well compensated, even if the financial elements of the relationship were not worked out until their divorce in 1996.

Diana was described by friends as being more content and calm shortly following the breakup. During a ski vacation in Colorado with personal trainer Jenny Rivett, who was shocked that the princess accepted her offer, she laughed readily and frequently. Rivett stated that Diana feared the prospect of spending the holidays apart from her husband, but she ended the trip by declaring that it had been one of her most joyous holidays ever.

Diana was wealthy, renowned, adored, and alone. And she was still in charge of the children she loved. She was 31 years old and anxious to see what life had to offer, both professionally and emotionally. Anthony Holden's cover story in the February 1993 issue of Vanity Fair, titled "Di's Palace Coup," described the difference between the Diana who was bound to Charles and the Diana who was suddenly free. Holden described a previously unknown bounce in her step and a brightness in her eye. Meanwhile, another publication had staked out her husband's reputation. The Camillagate tapes, which had only been seen to the British public in November, were published in their entirety a month earlier. Diana's image as a victim of Charles' adultery was cemented. She had always been the favorite of the two, both globally and in the United Kingdom, particularly among women. Despite the public's suspicions about her infidelity with Hewitt, the sensationally explicit sexual phone banter between Charles and Camilla in 1989 confirmed that he had gone headfirst into an affair.

Even if Charles and Diana had started their unfaithful relationships at the same time, the damage to the former would have been greater. After all, Charles had been nurtured in the royal family. Though he had no intention of making such indiscretions public, the fact that he had participated in such a lowbrow, sexually focused conversation shattered his ambition to be considered seriously. Charles desired recognition for his political and philosophical convictions. His stated fantasy of being transformed into a tampon so he could constantly be "close" to Camilla was not going to gain him that respect. To be sure, some well-known world leaders are likely to have engaged in adolescent sexual behavior, but they were not detected. And perception was everything in his instance. Such revelations just destroyed Charles.

Diana's reputation, on the other hand, suffered only minor damage. Her infidelity had not yet been verified, but her image had been cemented as a victim of Charles' supposed flippant attitude toward unfaithfulness and the misery he caused on her. Women rallied to her support, branding her a symbol of female victimhood. Diana eagerly absorbed everything. The happiness she felt on the skiing trip immediately after the split was disclosed persisted. She now felt free, as she was no longer bound by the limits in her daily routine that had previously been imposed on her by royal family traditions. She also particularly loved personalizing Kensington Apartments Eight and Nine.

Diana's entourage included butler Paul Burrell, whom she asked to accompany her to Kensington. The shock of the separation affected Burrell, who initially opposed the plan but subsequently became one of Diana's staunchest supporters. At Kensington, he was allowed to act with significantly less formality than he was at Highgrove. Visitors noticed a more relaxed and welcoming atmosphere, both in the way the house was designed and in how they were treated. The seductive sound of classical music and the perfume of sweet-smelling flowers greeted guests as they arrived. Diana lightened up Charles's dismal military art and structures with peaceful landscapes. "There was a lot more banter and laughter, and not so much creeping around," one companion explained. "Even the cleaners say hello."

Despite her best efforts to give Kensington her own spin, with a focus on making her sons feel at ease, something inside Diana pushed for a clean split. She began to crave for her own country house, free of all links to her royal heritage. Despite the fact that she was separated from Charles, she remained under the constant careful eyes of guards outside Kensington Palace, with a staff attending to her every need. She remembered her stay at Coleherne Court as carefree and enjoyable. She recognized that her personal and professional obligations had expanded enormously, but she still had a strong desire to cut her royal ties, at least in terms of her residence, and move into a smaller and less visible home. Her only concern was the inevitability of harsh criticism from the royal family, the media, and the British people for such an open departure from the royal life she had led for almost a decade. But no matter how hard she tried to make Kensington Palace her own, a horrible feeling flooded over her every time she returned from one of her increasingly frequent weekend visits to friends' houses. Every memento of the prince had been discarded or delivered to him at his new St. James residence, but the couple had spent so much time at Kensington Palace over the years that the unpleasant memories could not be erased. "I wake up on Sunday morning and I dread going back," Diana said to friends. "It's like returning to prison."

New Beau, but No New Residence

In April 1993, it appeared that her brother Charles was prepared to grant her a "get out of jail free" pass. He offered her the Garden House, a comparably modest four-bedroom property on the Althorp estate. Diana had been concerned about being perceived as lavish, especially now that she was merely a minor member of the royal family. That dread had even led her to sell her luxury Mercedes once the divorce was finalized. She was ecstatic at the prospect of decorating her own home for the first time in her life. After all, Kensington was hardly her own, and her Coleherne Court apartment had been shared with housemates. However, her brother determined that police surveillance and media interest would limit any hope of peace and quiet. Diana was furious at Charles for rejecting his offer without first consulting with her. She wrote two letters pleading with him to reconsider, but received no response. Diana had wasted a lot of time and effort planning her new home. Her relationship with her brother was strained for a long time after that happened.

Meanwhile, despite his marriage to French heiress Diane de Waldner, with whom Diana said he was no longer in love, her romance with gorgeous, debonair art dealer Oli-ver Hoare was heating up. According to critics, the princess began dating Hoare seriously because he was a close friend of Charles's and she was still seeking vengeance for her estranged husband's affair with Camilla. Hoare and the prince had many interests, including a love of art and literature. He shared another trait with Charles: a proclivity for adultery. He married Waldner in 1976, but had a protracted affair with a married Turkish woman named Ayesha Gul. In the mid-1980s, Hoare and his wife befriended Charles and Diana, as well as Andrew and Camilla Parker Bowles. Diana had developed more than a friendship with Hoare right before her divorce was finalized. Despite her efforts to conceal the relationship, Diana's protection officer Ken Wharfe stated that personnel at closely guarded Kensington Palace became aware of it when she attempted to sneak

Hoare in through the courtyard of Princess Margaret's apartment with a blanket over his head. They would meet for lunch at San Lorenzo in the afternoons, which was owned by a woman who offered up her adjoining apartment to them after meals. Diana and her new beau played cat and mouse with photographers who tried to photograph them. When asked about her relationship with a married man, Diana said Hoare vowed to leave his wife and flee to Italy with her to start a new life. Diana was smitten with the affluent art dealer, according to Wharfe. Simone Simmons, a close friend and healer, sought to persuade Diana that Hoare was only making empty promises. "He's going to marry me," declared the princess. "Yes, and pigs might fly," Simmons said.

Diana questioned whether she would ever find true and enduring love. Hoare would fail to produce it, adding to an already depressingly extensive list.

CHAPTER 11:
Still Pursuing My Dream

Diana was tenacious—too tenacious—in her quest to keep Hoare. She'd spoken with Hoare's wife, Diane, several times, claiming that her relationship with him was only a friendship. Diane, on the other hand, got concerned when the tone of their phone calls shifted. Diana became irritable, and the frequency of her phone calls increased, causing Diane to think that Oliver and the princess were having an affair. After all, hadn't he had a long-term sexual relationship with Gul? Diane did not directly confront her husband. She did, however, demand that he limit his time with Diana and inform her unequivocally that the phone calls must stop. Diana kept up the correspondence, calling three or four times a day and hanging up whenever Diane answered.

The princess begged Hoare to maintain their relationship not for the sake of physical contact, but for her emotional needs. They talked about his wife's fears, but Diana said, "Doesn't she understand what I'm going through?" Doesn't she realize I need your aid and advice with all of my horrible problems? ...Isn't Diane aware that I don't have anyone to whom I can turn? Is there no one I can rely on? You are my sole companion. Doesn't she see how miserable I am alone?"1 Hoare began to withdraw as a result of the pulling in two directions. The less Hoare saw of Diana, though, the more frantic she became and the more she called him. Her primary aim was to hear his calming voice, therefore she hardly spoke.

Diana's actions around Oliver Hoare were rightfully chastised. After all, hadn't she endured immense mental pain as a result of Charles' romance with Camilla? She was now Camilla in this relationship. Though it is speculated that Diana's problematic behavior was motivated by her enthusiasm over the new freedom provided by the separation, Diana did ask Hoare to honor his commitment to leave his wife. She joked early on about their virtually identical first names and how if Hoare shouted out her name in bed, his wife Diane would have no idea. But Diana soon grew overly protective of her beau and began insisting on exclusive rights to Hoare, sending him fleeing. He started skipping her regular commitments before he stopped seeing her entirely. Hoare also abandoned his wife for two months before returning.

In the fall of 1993, Diane got a particularly unpleasant phone call, which she assumed was made by Diana. Diane had been frightened and enraged by similar calls, but this one was very terrible, so she requested her husband call British Telecom to have the calls traced. Oliver Hoare granted her request, believing Diana would never have spoken so venomously to his wife. The phone company had a tracking device installed on the Hoares' phone. The calls halted for a few months, but on January 13, 1994, six calls were made. Other calls came in that week as well. Oliver Hoare was shown one number by British Telecom, which he immediately recognized as Diana's personal number at Kensington Palace. The police notified Buckingham Palace, and Diana was contacted by the queen's personal secretary, Robert Fellowes. The calls unexpectedly halted, causing Oliver and Diane Hoare to abandon the case.

The media, on the other hand, had a field day. After the News of the World published a story about Diana's phone calls to Hoare, she reacted aggressively to the reporters and photographers who surrounded her. Hoare told reporters that he and Diane both understood his connection with Diana was not unlawful, but the episode made Diana appear needy and petulant. She told a royal correspondent for the Daily Mail that she had been framed. "What are they trying to accomplish with me?"" she inquired. "I feel like I'm being annihilated. There is no truth to it." She also stated that, while she did call Hoare, the substance of the calls was not as described. Diana also opened her engagement book and pointed to multiple days when she was suspected of calling Hoare, but she claimed that her location would have made it impossible. She eventually admitted to acquaintance Joseph Sanders that she had made the calls, not just from her home, but also from various phone booths while disguised. Though many members of the British public believed Diana harassed Diane Hoare, many blamed her weak emotional state after their divorce.

Diana was soon to be demonized for another previous relationship. Hewitt was the man in question, and by 1994, he was attempting to cash in on his connection with Diana. When notified of audio recordings and images in newspaper safes that would link him to the princess, Hewitt became terrified. Despite having distinguished himself as a brave and effective soldier during the Gulf War, reports regarding their connection had played a role in his deteriorating military career. He needed the money, and both tabloids and publishers were willing to give it to him. Hewitt quickly met with Daily Express journalist Diana Pasternak to learn what the media was up to, but the strategy failed. Not only did he learn nothing, but he also learnt a lot about his affair with Diana. Hewitt soon discovered that the author was hard at work on a book about the relationship called Princess in Love, which would be released in time for the holiday shopping season. Though his accusations of a sexual relationship with Diana were plastered all over the newspapers, the press consistently called Hewitt a money-grubbing cad. Most people thought that as a representative of the British military, he should have had a sense of honor that would have kept him from tarnishing the reputation of a woman in line to be queen.

Diana was understandably concerned when Pasternak's book was out. But she did more than sigh with relief when she saw a headline in the October 8, 1994, edition of the Daily Mirror claiming Diana was blameless for her conduct. She gave out a happy yell. According to the same newspaper's study, only 27% of its readers blamed Diana for her affair with Hewitt, and only 15% said the princess's reputation had been harmed. Surprisingly, 81% believed Charles had driven her into the arms of another man, and 61% suggested the pair divorce immediately. The monarchy's reputation has also suffered as a result of the publicity. A troubling 73% of people polled believed Queen Elizabeth II should be the final British monarch.

Charles' Point of View

Hewitt was not the only man in Diana's life who sparked debate. In early 1994, British television personality Jonathan Dimbleby was working on a documentary and a biography on Prince Charles, both of which he believed would vindicate him after all of the allegations regarding his treatment of Diana in Andrew Morton's book. Diana became more concerned about the contents of the work, despite Dimbleby's efforts to reassure her during a meeting in March. The filmed interview between Dimbleby and the prince praised his work in that job, but the most notable moment was Charles's response to claims of infidelity before the separation. The prince maintained that the charges that he was habitually unfaithful were incorrect, and that he strayed only when both he and the princess saw the marriage as an irreversible failure, albeit he did not mention Camilla Parker Bowles. The documentary, which broadcast on June 29th, was seen by 63% of the British viewing public. Diana was among those who didn't watch, instead attending a fund-raising event at a London gallery in a revealing, sensual black gown that stole part of the documentary's thunder in media stories the next day. However, the princess eventually admitted to having taped the Dimbleby interview with her divorced spouse.

Charles was moved by both the television show and the book. Despite the fact that they showed indiscretions in her personal life, Diana learned with great joy that she was still loved in the United

Kingdom and around the world. Since the separation was announced, this had been the situation. She was no longer required to show an emotional link to Charles during solo travels to Zimbabwe and Nepal in early 1993. She preferred to serve as a British ambassador rather than as a representative of the royal family. She became more involved with the International Red Cross and worked to raise awareness about AIDS and poverty in developing countries. She kept working with the homeless. Land mine abolition became a favorite project as well. Diana even worked with ladies who had suffered from eating disorders, like she had.

Despite being extremely successful, her journey to Zimbabwe was quite frustrating. Diana was struck with emotion on a visit to an AIDS hospice for children. She sobbed when she realized that none of the children would live to the age of six. Later in the trip, photos of Diana leaning over a giant pot and handing out food to hungry children were rather poignant, but she knew she would soon return to her life of riches and ease, while these same children were bound to severe poverty. Those close to her, once again, noticed her genuine concern for the predicament of those considerably less fortunate. "Those who believe Diana's work was nothing more than a series of photo opportunities in glamor-ous locations around the world should have seen this drained, exhausted woman sitting in the back of the helicopter that day and heard her speak of the heart-breaking scenes she had just witnessed," Ken Wharfe3 said.

She tried to immerse herself in her career, even enrolling in public speaking classes to improve her efficacy. Diana recruited veteran soap opera actor Peter Settelin, who trained her how to converse more effectively. She utilized the advice during an April 1993 address on eating disorders at Kensington Town Hall, during which her more personable approach nearly resulted in a full-fledged admission of her fight with bulimia. Diana had become a champion of women's concerns at that point, having visited a domestic abuse shelter a month before. In June of that year, she also spoke at a symposium in support of mentally ill women.

However, Diana's hectic schedule, unfavorable media attention, and other distractions began to catch up with her. Even before the events of 1994, she was despondent. She was continually concerned about poor media coverage, which kept her awake at night. Diana even employed a sleep therapist, who controlled her oxygen intake to ensure a good night's sleep. She was not only fatigued, but also suffering from numbing headaches, all of which put her in a bad attitude. Diana became irritated and impatient with paparazzi, or freelance photographers who trailed her every step and sold their photographs to the highest bidder. She tried to flee, but instead of following the advice of others who suggested she take her children to a peaceful place, Diana took them to Disney World. She expected to be lost in the crowd, but she was mistaken. Throughout the journey, photographers followed her and her sons. When Diana returned to Kensington Palace, media headlines chastised her for spending money on a lavish vacation while leading philanthropic efforts to help starving children.

Another swell in Diana's life after her divorce came from Prince Charles, who employed Alexandra "Tiggy" Legge-Bourke as a "surrogate mother" for William and Harry when they were not in Diana's care. The princess was enraged when she saw newspaper photos of her younger son sitting on Legge-Bourke's knees. Diana and Camilla both detested Legge-Bourke, who believed that the princes required what she was offering, such as a gun and a horse, rather than their mother's tennis racquet and bucket of popcorn at the movies. Diana not only saw Camilla as a threat to her motherhood, the only realm in which Charles and the royal family had not interfered, but she also suspected her of having an affair with her estranged husband. Indeed, several at Buckingham Palace thought Legge-Bourke would make an excellent wife for the prince.

Privacy Invasion

One incident in November persuaded Diana to make dramatic adjustments in her public life. She opened the Sunday Mirror one morning to find a full-page photograph of herself working out at a health club in a tight leotard. Club manager Bryce Taylor was paid a large quantity of money to hand over the images to the publication. It was determined that the photograph had been taken without her awareness using a camera hidden in the ceiling. It showed her rowing on a machine with her legs stretched wide apart. Diana filed a lawsuit against the newspaper and settled before the matter went to trial, assuring that the images would never be published again. One might expect a response against such media manipulation, but none came, even after Taylor accused Diana of having a secret wish to have such images shot. The incident convinced Diana that the tabloid press's ambition to sell papers without regard for the truth was stronger than her capacity to prevent it. Diana was also inspired to make the decision to retire from public life.

This decision was made on December 3, 1993, during a meeting of the Headway National Head Injuries Association. Diana spoke emotionally and with conviction, despite her shaking voice, and requested "time and space" before proceeding with her explanation. "When I started my public life 12 years ago, I understood that the media might be interested in what I did," she told those in attendance. "I realized at the time that their focus would inevitably be on both our private and public lives." But I had no idea how overwhelming that attention would become, or how much it would damage both my official obligations and my personal life in a way that has been difficult to bear."4 She then spoke about her sons as her first priority before leaving to a standing ovation.

Diana spent much of 1994 trying to find herself after her public engagement calendar was unexpectedly cleared. In order to find peace and fulfillment, she sought the advice of numerous healers, astrologers, psychics, and other gurus. She went to masseurs and acupuncturists to treat her physique. Diana and astrologer Debbie Frank were sitting on the carpet, surrounded by zodiac charts, following the movements of the planets, according to Paul Burrell. "You really need to have your chart read," Diana pleaded with Burrell. "It's riveting stuff." Despite her great belief in the therapeutic benefits of such out-of-the-way activities, Diana demonstrated an ability to laugh at both them and herself for her participation.

Susie Orbach, a specialist in eating disorders who eventually tamed Diana's bulimia, which she continued to suffer from until the 1990s, administered one round of therapies to Diana. Orbach published Fat Is a Feminist Issue in 1978, claiming that women's fixation with their weight is the product of men who control relationships. It's no surprise Diana was drawn to its contents—her drive to lose weight was fueled by a desire to look attractive enough to entice Charles away from Camilla. Despite Diana's friendship with healer Simone Simmons in the 1990s, Orbach proved to be her most essential mentor. She not only assisted Diana in overcoming her bulimia, but she also instructed her on how to create a more favorable relationship with Charles and the royal family. She even helped Diana prepare for a national televised interview with Panorama correspondent Martin Bashir in 1995.

Diana required assistance. Despite the fact that she had been separated for nearly two years and had had relationships with other men, her hatred for Charles had not subsided. She suffered as much emotional sorrow as she had at any moment throughout their 12-year relationship when the prince said in a television appearance with Dimbleby that he never loved her. And Diana was far from finished with his romance with Camilla. She told a friend that visions of the two together in her head during a highway trip resulted in furious wrath. "I felt mesmerized, unable to focus on anything but Charles and Camilla," Diana explained. "I could see them kissing, making love, eating together, riding out together, listening to music together, doing everything together while I was alone with the boys driving them to school." I drove with tears welling up in my eyes. But my heart was filled with rage and hatred."

Diana also had some harsh words for Charles' admission that he had never loved her, not only in relation to herself, but also in relation to his boys. "How could he say such a thing?"" she inquired. "Didn't he realize it was terrible for the boys to hear about their father and mother's relationship?" Making that statement revealed Charles to be a selfish jerk, as if nothing in the world mattered except his feelings—not his wife, his children, or any of their memories. I would gladly have scratched his eyes out for let the world know."

Camilla revealed her impending divorce from Andrew Parker Bowles shortly after. For a long time, it had been a marriage of convenience—he was well aware of her relationship with Charles and had no shortage of female companions of his own. Diana, on the other hand, believed that Camilla's single status would allow her to freely express her feelings for the prince and spend more time with William and Harry. Camilla was quickly revealed to be Charles' mistress, therefore ending any possibility of a royal marriage reconciliation. Diana was summoned for a meeting with the queen and Prince Philip, who chastised the princess for her previous behavior and threatened to depose her title if she did not change.

Her recent behavior included a liaison with Will Carling, a gorgeous and married British rugby star who functioned as her unofficial personal trainer. Despite neither admitting to actual encounters, other publications have argued that the connection was sexual in nature. Julia Carling, Carling's wife, told reporters that the princess was destroying their marriage, and her husband promised never to visit Diana again. Soon after, he was spotted bringing rugby clothes to William and Harry at Kensington Palace, prompting the Carlings to announce their divorce. Julia approached the media once more, this time with a finger pointing squarely at Diana. Will Carling refused to reveal the nature of his relationship with the princess in his autobiography written several years later. Many in the media suspected the two had sexual encounters, and many blamed Diana for the marriage's demise. Today posed the question, "Is Will Carling just another trophy for the bored, manipulative, and selfish princess?"", while the Daily Express wondered, "Is no marriage or man safe from the wife of the heir to the throne?"”

Uncensored Diana

Diana argued that her connection with Carling was platonic and that it had stopped when the story broke in the tabloids, but her damaged reputation drove her to prepare a candid interview with Bashir on Panorama, the most recognized news program on British television. The interview aired on November 14, 1995, Prince Charles's 47th birthday, and was watched by an estimated 23 million British viewers. Diana candidly answered questions on a wide range of topics, including Charles, the royal family, her battles with bulimia, Gilbey, Hoare, and her responsibilities as Princess of Wales. The following were some of the interview's highlights:

On reaction to her postnatal depression: “It gave everybody a won-derful new label—Diana’s unstable and Diana’s mentally unbal-anced. And unfortunately that seems to have stuck on and off over the years.”

On her bulimia: “You inflict it upon yourself because your self-esteem is at a low ebb, and you don’t think you’re worthy or valuable. . . . It was a symptom of what was going on in my mar-riage. I was crying out for help, but giving the wrong signals."

On Camilla's role in the failure of her marriage: "Well, there were three of us in this marriage, so it was a bit crowded."

On royal family treatment since the separation: "People's agendas changed overnight. I was now the separated wife of the Prince of Wales. I had a problem. I was a liability, and how are we going to deal with her?"

On her relationship with Hewitt: "He was a great friend of mine at a very difficult, yet another difficult time, and he was always there to support me, and I was absolutely devastated when this book appeared, because I trusted him. . . . There was a lot of fan-tasy in that book, and it was very distressing for me that a friend of mine, who I had trusted, made money out of me."

On whether she had been unfaithful to Charles: "Yes, I adored (Hewitt). Yes, I was in love with him."

On a typical day regarding paparazzi: "When I have my public duties, I understand that when I get out of the car I'm being photographed, but actually it's now when I get out of my door, my front door, I'm being photographed. I never know where a lens is going to be. A normal day would be followed by four cars, a normal day would be to come back to my car and find six freelance photographers jumping around me."

On how she perceives her role: "The biggest disease this world suffers from in this day and age is the disease of people feeling unloved, and I know that I can give love for a minute, for half an hour, for a day, for a month, but I can give—I'm very happy to do that and I want to do that."

The interview went over like ripped pants at a royal gala at Buckingham Palace. Diana told Bashir that the royal family did not allow her to mature as a person, that they gave her little credit for her achievements, and that they undercut her status as Princess of Wales after their divorce. Dickie Arbiter, Charles's private secretary, stated the broadcast was greeted "like a cup of cold sickness." To be honest, we were taken aback. Nobody saw it coming." Even her mother, Frances Shand Kydd, whose relationship with the princess had deteriorated, chastised her daughter, calling the interview a "frightful mistake" and a "total error of judgment."

The general population had a quite different opinion. According to a Daily Mirror poll, an astounding 92 percent of people who replied supported Diana's words during the interview. According to a national opinion poll sponsored by the Sunday Times, two-thirds of the British public praised the interview, and a slightly greater percentage thought Diana should be appointed as a goodwill ambassador abroad. Soon after the interview, she traveled to the United States to accept a Humanitarian of the Year award from the United Cerebral Palsy Foundation of New York, cementing her reputation in her own nation. The award was given to her by none other than former Secretary of State Henry Kissinger.

Her nefarious side

Diana may have felt invincible as a result of the outpouring of popular support. This explains her one-sided altercation with Legge-Bourke at the Lanesborough Hotel on Hyde Park Corner following her return from New York. She told Paul Burrell to keep an eye on her, then strolled over to her children's nanny, whom she believed had become more than just Charles' aide. "Good day, Tiggy." "How are you doing?" Diana said with a knowing smile. "Sorry to hear about the baby." The insinuation was that she became pregnant with the prince's kid and had the pregnancy terminated. Legge-Bourke bolted left the room, and Diana turned to Burrell, saying, "Did you see the look on her face, Paul? She almost passed out!" Charles and the queen were both enraged. Diana's scathing charges not only forced Legge-Bourke to seek attorneys in order to write a statement refuting them, but they also proved to be the final straw for the royal family in accepting Diana and the current arrangement. An investigation discovered that Legge-Bourke had visited her private gynecologist twice in the fall of 1995, as well as checked into a hospital, but there was no indication of what the princess had charged. Diana was asked to apologize, but she declined. Both Charles and the queen had pressed on a quick divorce by that point.

An outsider may imagine that such a prospect would send Diana into a tailspin. After all, three years had passed since their divorce, and while she had yet to meet the man who would offer her fulfillment, she demonstrated with surety that she was open to new experiences. Furthermore, one would think that her rage at Charles for his affair with Camilla, as well as his admission on public television that he never loved her in the first place, ruled out the idea of a divorce. Those close to Diana, however, feel she still loved Prince Charles and couldn't bear the end of her connection with him. Yes, she had threatened him with divorce several times while they were together, but mainly to draw his attention to the problems in their marriage, primarily his infidelity.

But there it was: a letter from the queen herself, dated December 18, 1995, advising that Diana and Charles divorce for the first time. It wasn't Diana's idea of getting into the Christmas spirit, but the queen had had enough of the media circus centered on their adulterous romances and petty fighting to allow it to continue. After all, she wondered, what possible explanation could they have offered for remaining married? Diana was irritated by the letter, and she protested to Burrell that the queen had discussed the matter with authorities such as Prime Minister John Major and the Archbishop of Canterbury before reaching her in such an impersonal fashion as a letter from Windsor Castle. Under the circumstances, Diana was unconcerned about the national ramifications of her public breakup with Charles. How did it influence her and her sons, rather? She believed that such a personal, emotional matter should be treated as such, rather than as a business choice. However, the letter was not drafted in a businesslike manner. The queen merely stated that a divorce would only exacerbate the harm already done to William and Harry.

Diana wasted little time calling the queen, whom she kindly persuaded to give the topic further contemplation, as promised in return. The princess then wrote a letter to the queen requesting additional time. The next day, though, Charles sent a letter declaring unequivocally his desire for a divorce, which he considered was unavoidable. Surprisingly, a comparison of the prince's letter and that of the queen revealed identical portions, causing Diana to believe that the plot for an immediate divorce had been devised by both of them. She then scribbled a note to her estranged husband, claiming uncertainty and refusing to agree to the divorce.

While struggling to keep her husband, Diana lost her private secretary, P. D. Jephson, who resigned in January 1996. He had been a faithful aide, but her cruel statements to Legge-Bourke, along with press reports that Diana was seeking a divorce, convinced Jephson that he could no longer stay with Diana. "My boss's treatment of Tiggy was all that my wavering resolve needed," Jephson writes in his autobiography. "Later, rather than sooner, I discovered that loyalty to the Princess now conflicted with a higher loyalty—namely, basic decency." In light of the Queen's letter suggesting divorce, I concluded that if I stood up for the Princess as I should, I would undoubtedly be at odds with the head of state."

The media's coverage of the queen's letter effectively ended the royal marriage. Diana saw the queen at Buckingham Palace on February 15, 1996, the day after she sent Charles a Valentine's Day card. Still troubled by envy, Diana asked the queen if she thought the prince was fated to marry Camilla, to which Diana received the reassuring response that it was highly unlikely. She told the queen unequivocally that she did not want the divorce and that she was still in love with Charles, adding that she was entirely to blame for the tragic situation. Diana believed that the queen and the Duke of Edinburgh had worked hard to keep the marriage together, but she did not give Charles the same credit. When they met two weeks later to discuss the divorce, she did, according to friends, assure her soon-to-be ex-husband that she would always love him.

Among the topics debated was whether Diana would still be addressed as "Her Royal Highness." It was agreed that she would be known as "Diana, Princess of Wales." Diana told associates she was offended by the semantic shift, while Buckingham Palace officials insisted it was her idea. Diana received the equivalent of $2.2 million in a lump amount, as well as approximately $600,000 each year to manage her office, as part of the divorce settlement. Despite the loss of her title, she would still be regarded as a member of the royal family. On August 28, the marriage was officially dissolved.

Diana was never the type to swoon over money. She had grown up in an aristocratic household and had grown accustomed to a royal lifestyle, so the idea of being in financial need was unfamiliar to her. But the idea of being in emotional distress was all too familiar. It would accompany her until her death, a sad incident that proved tragically near.

CHAPTER 12:
The Last Years and the Fatal End

Diana covered her pain skillfully, even when the ink on her divorce papers was hardly dry. In fact, friends and members of the media remarked that she had never looked or felt better. She was afraid that the end of her marriage would crush her emotionally, but it instead elevated her spirits and relieved her burden. In her more careless moments, she feigned disinterest in her ex-husband's connection with Camilla, even expressing a desire for the two to marry so that his former mistress could take care of William and Harry.

Diana reduced her staff significantly, giving Paul Burrell numerous tasks, including acting as a shoulder to weep on when needed. However, he was not required in this capacity immediately following the divorce. She was striving for a clean break, which provoked another—the smashing of all her Princess of Wales crockery with a hammer. She then stated that with the money Charles was providing, she could buy anything.

The princess also restricted her charitable contributions to the six organizations she was most enthusiastic about: Centrepoint (for homeless young people), the Royal Marsden Hospital, Great Ormond Street Hospital for Children, the English National Ballet, the Leprosy Mission, and the National AIDS Trust. Aside from the ballet, which she appreciated on a more personal basis, Diana sought to learn more about the needs of her charity without being viewed as a royal family figurehead. By reducing the number of charities in which she was involved, she was able to address those concerns more thoroughly. Meanwhile, Diana was busy fortifying friendships, the most important of which were with Tiffany's president, Rosa Monckton, Brazilian ambassador Lucia Flecha de Lima, and Lady Annabel Goldsmith, whom she saw as a trustworthy mother figure. Diana had close relationships with this group, which allowed her to socialize more. So did Cosima Somerset, who had recently split up with her husband, Lord John Somerset, and with whom Diana felt a great deal of empathy due to their practically identical experiences and bleak future prospects.

Cosima got a terrifying insight into Diana's daily fight with the paparazzi in May 1996. The two had made an instructive journey to Ma-jorca, where they bared their souls, sharing their lives from childhood through divorce. They were pursued by paparazzi on automobiles and motorcycles as their hotel manager drove them over the twisting mountain roads. One of them drove dangerously close to them, his camera lens inches from the car window. Diana remained cool; she was used to such invasions of her private life. Cosima was taken aback not only by the lone paparazzo's bravery, but also by her friend's calm reaction to the occurrence.

Following her separation from Charles, Diana's latest love interest was Pakistani heart surgeon Hasnat Khan. In fact, they spent the night together at Kensington Palace just hours after the divorce was finalized. She'd known Khan for about a year at that point, but the public scrutiny and accompanying response from her prior relationships had prompted her to take her time with Khan, despite her admiration for him. Khan was working on his PhD at the Brompton Hospital in London when he aided in heart surgery for Joe Toffolo, Diana's acu-puncturist's husband. Toffolo's health and upcoming operation piqued the princess's interest, as she had always been captivated by the subject of medicine. When Khan walked into the room and into her life, her interest surged exponentially. In opposition to her very shallow connections with Hewitt and Hoare, her intellectual interest in him went much deeper. Khan piqued her interest not only in Islam, which she considered converting to, but also in spiritual topics concerning life and death. Diana frequently spent hours visiting patients in the hospital while Khan was at work.

She spent so much time with Khan at the hospital that she had to disguise herself, complete with a long, dark wig, to avoid drawing attention to herself. The pseudonym was so effective that she started using it for everyday tasks.

Diana ultimately invited Hasnat to Kensington Palace for supper to meet William and Harry. She was certain that Hasnat would be her life companion. She had met a man who would be supportive of her and with whom she had built a multidimensional relationship for the first time. His independence, though, hindered the closeness she required. Diana requested that Hasnat relocate to Kensington Palace, but he refused. He even turned down a cell phone, which would have allowed Diana to contact him at the regularity she demanded. Undaunted, she continued leaving messages on his pager and dialing the hospital switchboard with a false name and an urgent need to reach him. Khan soon became tired of the act, but it wasn't until the public learned of their relationship in November 1996 that Khan backed down. Ironically, her determination to advance his profession and begin their life together proved to be their undoing. Diana visited Dr. Christian Barnard, who conducted the world's first heart transplant in 1967, when in Italy to accept one of numerous humanitarian prizes. She requested that Barnard locate Khan's work in South Africa, where they could establish a home. The romance and Diana's desire to be his wife were shortly reported by the Daily Mirror.

Hasnat, a private guy, was enraged by the media and annoyed with the princess for interfering with his business life. He was even more outraged when Diana told Daily Mail reporter Richard Kay that the story was untrue, although knowing it to be real. Khan was also offended that Diana would discount a tale about her feelings for him. The incident prompted Khan to cut off connection with Diana for several weeks, which greatly distressed her. Tears that had not been shed since the divorce was finalized returned. The couple eventually reconciled, albeit only for a short time. Hasnat was put off by the obvious notoriety that a relationship with Diana would bring. Diana persisted in her pursuit despite learning from Hasnat's friends that if they married, she would be destined to live with his family in Pakistan, where she would not have the responsibilities she'd grown accustomed to as a princess and would be denied the freedom that women in Western culture take for granted. Even so, she was undeterred. Her passion for him affected her judgment to the point where she traveled to Pakistan without his knowledge in May 1997 to meet with his parents. His mother, Naheed, objected to her son's involvement with a fashionable British woman, while Hasnat was enraged by Diana's activities and what he saw to be her attempts to dominate his life. The marriage was doomed.

New Advertising Campaign

The divorce from the royal family separated two Dianas: the emotionally fragile woman who searched vainly, often with utter disregard for others, for the perfect man and personal fulfillment, and the strong, caring princess who achieved humanitarian greatness by bringing hope and positive change to the lives of those less fortunate. Late in 1996, Michael Whit-lam, Director General of the British Red Cross, began sending Diana images and reports of the devastation caused by landmines laid during WWII but never cleared. Though Diana had dropped the Red Cross from her list of charitable organizations, Whitlam believed the moment had come for her to take on the cause. She traveled to the African country of Angola in mid-January 1997. Fifteen million landmines had been placed across the war-torn country of only 12 million people, with 70,000 of them stepping on one. As a result, an estimated 40,000 people were amputated, with few having their limbs restored.

Upon her arrival in Angola, she immediately declared a campaign to assist the Red Cross in eliminating the use of anti landmines around the world, which contradicted official British policy and drew condemnation from Tory Party political figures. Diana was surprised by the lack of respect for what she was seeking to do, prompting Prime Minister John Major to declare his support, arguing that the prohibition of land mines was in accordance with the British government's ultimate goal. Diana got additional backing after being observed valiantly trudging over minefields in the highly mined hamlet of Cuito. When reporters playfully asked her to repeat the perilous excursion, she astonished everyone by agreeing. She also garnered affection and respect by cheering on specialists embarking on a perilous mine-clearing mission and, in classic Diana flair, comforting a youngster dying from injuries sustained in a land mine mishap. She wrapped a blanket around her and massaged her hand as she spoke gently to her. "Who was that?" the toddler inquired of Sunday Times international correspondent Christina Lamb.``, to which Lamb replied, "She's a princess from England, from far away," to which the child replied, "Is she an angel?"" That afternoon, the child died from her wounds.``

Diana's popularity and influence were underlined by the mine dispute. Her anti-landmine stance was backed not only by Labour Opposition Leader Tony Blair and other liberal politicians, but also by powerful military officials such as US General Norman Schwarzkopf and his British equivalent Sir Peter de la Billiere. Diana had established herself as a humanitarian years before and was never one to be concerned with politics. Her trip to Angola, however, shook British politics. Tory officials hurried to Diana's side after realizing the damage done by their criticism of her support for a land mine prohibition, but it was too late. A few months later, the party was soundly defeated in the general election, handing the government to the opposition for the first time since 1979. Blair, 44, was elected prime minister with the biggest margin of victory in a British election in the twentieth century, ushering in an age of youth, vibrancy, and new ideas in British politics. Diana was believed to fit in well with such principles, and the land mine scandal was seen as a crucial factor in the Tory government's demise. "How dare anyone criticize Diana Princess of Wales for taking up this heartrend-ing cause," commented Clare Short, Secretary of State for International Development. "Diana's stance on the issue deserves high praise." Her public prominence can offer millions of victims and campaigners hope that there will be a global ban on the manufacture and use of anti-personnel landmines once and for all."

Meanwhile, Diana appeared to be treading on an emotional land mine with each man she sought. Her assertiveness contributed to her expulsion of Hasnat Khan, whose flattery at the prospect of a beautiful princess falling in love with him was offset by his rage at her intrusions into his personal life and the consequent tremendous publicity. In June 1997, she attended the Khan family on their annual vacation to Stratford-upon-Avon, when it became clear that her upbringing and history just did not allow her to blend in with the Muslim family. When the affair between Khan and Diana was revealed to the public, he confided in a friend, who advised him to quit the relationship. Khan adored Diana, but his ultimate goal in life was to become a doctor and return to his native Pakistan. Diana's personal life had reached a new low when he informed her that it was finished. Diana no longer spoke to her mother, despite the fact that she had momentarily built an acceptable post marital relationship with Charles, with whom she got along well during occasions involving their children. Frances not only had a drinking problem, but she had also spoken out against her daughter's connection with Khan because of his race and religion, prompting the princess to cut all contact with her. Letters of apology were written to Diana but were returned unopened.

She also grew estranged from William and Harry, who had embraced the tough lifestyle encouraged by their father, Camilla, and Legge-Bourke. During their school vacations, they preferred hunting and exploring the wilds or racing around the go-kart track at Balmoral to being chased by the paparazzi at Disney World or hanging out at the vast houses owned by their mother's acquaintances. William, in particular, had become close to the royal family, particularly the queen and the Duke of Edinburgh. He regarded his des-tiny as the future monarch of England with zeal.

Diana's relationship with Charles also suffered a setback. It came to an end when Mark Bolland, who had been engaged in 1996 to help the prince's gravely damaged public image, began working to put Camilla in a favorable light. After her divorce, which was caused by Charles' public admission of an affair with her, the prince's mistress had taken a financial hit. Bolland believed that financing Camilla's recuperation would be a good public relations move for Charles, demonstrating responsibility toward the woman in his life. Camilla purchased a new property, replete with employees and a separate cottage for Scotland Yard security. Charles financed the majority of the costs, including Camilla's annual salary. And when Charles chose Highgrove for Camilla's 50th birthday party on July 17, 1997, Diana's bitterness and envy resurfaced. After all, Charles was now flaunting his affection for the lady who had tormented the princess—in their former house, no less—while Diana was unable to find any love at all. Bolland also prepared for a nice television documentary about Camilla, which Diana couldn't help but watch despite knowing it would bring her deep pain. After the show aired, the princess revealed her anguish to astrologer and friend Debbie Frank.

Paris's Last Tango

Diana planned to go on a trip to escape her pain, as she had done previously. She accepted an invitation to accompany her sons to the home of Egyptian multimillionaire Mohammed Al-Fayed, his wife Heini, and three of their youngest children in the south of France. The owner of London's Harrods department store had known the

Spencer family for years and was close to Diana's late father and second wife Raine. Al-Fayed, who was captivated by royalty and the lives they lead, had learnt about Diana's problems from Raine. His invitation, which had previously been declined, was extended solely to give the princess peace of mind. When she arrived, she discovered that Al-Fayed had spent $15 million on a 200-foot yacht dubbed the Janikal for the princess. And he eventually supplied his eldest son Dodi, a carousing playboy and marginally notable director with a well-publicized cocaine addiction who was engaged to marry American model Kelly Fisher, for companionship.

Diana's first impression of the Fayed family was favorable. Though she admonished a swarm of media people who had been tipped off about her vacation, demanding them to leave her alone, she genuinely enjoyed jet-skiing and swimming with her sons, as well as simply relaxing in Fayed's guarded property. But it was getting to know Dodi, who had been intimately associated with not only Fisher, but also well-known American models and actresses such as Brooke Shields, Cathy Lee Crosby, and Julia Roberts, that she appreciated the most. Though Dodi appeared to be a superficial hedonist on the surface, Diana dug deeper to learn more about him. Among her discoveries was that Dodi and Charles shared a need for significance in their lives, as well as an inner grief and sensitivity. Diana was drawn to Dodi's fragility, something she had always found appealing. And the affection was mutual. Dodi not only showed genuine concern for the princess, but also actively participated in her connection with William and Harry. Dodi booked a disco for two nights so she and her sons could dance alone. The gang also went to a nearby amusement park, where they raced in bumper cars. Diana enjoyed that Dodi didn't seem to regard the boys as mere distractions in his pursuit of her. Many people believe that friendship is a vital prerequisite for a love relationship.

But, could Dodi have remade Diana as "the princess bride"? Paul Burrell, his right-hand guy, didn't think so. Diana's sentiments for the jet-setter struck him as more of an infatuation than anything resembling love. His generosity and spontaneity took her away. Dodi invited her to travel to Paris for a dinner date soon after she returned from the South of France. She dialed Burrell's number from her hotel room, filled with excitement. Dodi had presented her with a gorgeous gold watch encircled by diamonds, she exclaimed. They returned to the Janikal a week later for a Mediterranean voyage.

Diana then traveled on a humanitarian trip to the former Yugoslavia and Bosnia to continue her efforts to rid the world of antipersonnel landmines. During the trip, she met Americans Jerry White and Ken Rutherford, who established the Landmine Survivors Network after becoming civilian victims of landmines. White was the only one who still had a leg. As the group, which included Burrell and Daily Telegraph reporter Bill Deedes, drove to Sarajevo, the two Americans discussed their accidents, and Diana responded, "My accident was on July 29, 1981," referring to her wedding day. After a brief pause, the people in the group realized the joke and burst out laughing.

Among the victims Diana met in Sarajevo was a 15-year-old girl who lived in a deplorable home without her parents. An exploding landmine blew off the girl's leg as she rummaged through a pile of trash for meager morsels of food for her two younger brothers. The princess observed the teenager's malnourished four-year-old sister lying on a foul-smelling mattress in the corner of a rear room as the media focused on that victim. The extremely mentally challenged child's eyes were closed and she was saturated in her own pee. Diana approached her and scooped her up, cradling her and caressed her arms and legs. The girl opened her eyes, revealing that she, too, lacked pupils and was blind. "I witnessed something very special," stated Burrell in his book. "A simple act of humanity, an act that personified the woman I knew so well."4 Diana was scheduled to visit Cambodia and Vietnam that October, giving her another chance to demonstrate her empathy for the less fortunate and her hatred of land mines, which had taken so many lives. But her life was cut short before she had the chance.

As Diana began her final three weeks on Earth, it appeared that her mother's prediction, which she had scornfully dismissed, was coming true. The loss of the title "Her Royal Highness" had allowed her to grow as a person and really increased her value. Diana's innate ability to relate with others, as well as her genuine compassion for individuals in the world in desperate need of assistance, were qualities that her loss of royal status could not take away. And now she was free to pursue causes of personal interest as well as what she saw as the most important issues confronting humanity. Diana was never afraid to take controversial views, and as a putative princess, she no longer had to worry about blowback. The British public remained so captivated with her that political figures raced to her side in all her humanitarian endeavors, as her stance on landmines demonstrated. Soon after her trek across Angola's minefields, 122 countries agreed to ban antipersonnel personnel mines, and the campaign that her name and compassion brought to the world's attention was awarded the Nobel Peace Prize. Diana was ready to transition from beloved princess to crucial international figure.

That is, until the early morning hours of August 31, 1997.

A Princess's Life Comes to an End

As the previous day began, there was still some ambiguity about Diana's feelings for Dodi. Despite the fact that Diana's companion Simone Simmons stated the princess never felt romantically close to Dodi and that the two never consummated their relationship, Diana told friends that she adored him and that Dodi had offered her great happiness. However, any relationship involving the princess drew the attention of tabloid reporters. The paparazzi trailed the pair, especially while they were relaxing on the 200-foot yacht. Diana wasn't bothered by those instances. After all, what could it hurt to have her photo shot from hundreds of feet away? And she didn't mind if photos of her lounging on the Janikal were published in newspapers all over the world. They depicted her as calm and content. Diana was extremely enraged when the paparazzi pursued her and invaded her personal space.

The pair intended to spend the night in Paris at Dodi's apartment after spending time at the Ritz's Imperial Suite. Philippe Dourneau, Dodi's personal chauffeur, was driving them out from the hotel in a Mercedes limousine, followed by two security officers in a Range Rover. They arrived at their destination only to be forced to fight their way past a swarm of paparazzi to the front door of Dodi's apartment building. Two hours later, they headed for their dinner reservations at the posh Chez Benoit, where they were once again followed by cameras. Dodi was so agitated by the crowd that he directed his chauffeur to return them to the Ritz. Cameras were placed within inches of Diana's face upon their arrival. Despite being irritated, she had become accustomed to such assaults of her private life. Dodi, on the other hand, was shaken by the event. They chose to enjoy their supper upstairs in their suite due to the attention they received while inside the restaurant. That's when Dodi devised a strategy to get rid of the paparazzi. He would tell the limo and Range Rover drivers to start their engines, fooling the paparazzi into thinking they were leaving by the front door when they were actually leaving through the back door into another car.

The maneuver did not produce the expected result. Though the majority of the paparazzi waited in front, a handful remained behind the Ritz. Diana and Dodi hopped into the backseat of a hired Mercedes that had come up around 12:20 a.m. Bodyguard Trevor

Rees-Jones and driver Henri Paul, an assistant security director at the Ritz, screamed at the paparazzi, "Don't bother following—you won't catch us."5 With paparazzi in cars and motorcycles chasing, the Mercedes traveled at speeds ranging from 90 to 122 miles per hour into the Alma Tunnel, which has a posted speed limit of 30 miles per hour. Seconds later, the Mercedes collided with a pillar before spinning across two lanes and hit a wall, brutally flinging the passengers. Romuald Rat, a 25-year-old paparazzo, was the first to arrive at the disaster site, leaping from his truck, aiming his camera at the tangled, twisted catastrophe, and snapping three photos that he would sell to the Sun as a one-day exclusive for nearly $500,000. Rat unlocked the Mercedes' rear car door and understood immediately that Dodi and Paul were no longer alive. Rees-Jones had survived multiple injuries despite being the only passenger who had worn a seatbelt. Diana was lying on her back, her head wedged between the two front seats, scarcely breathing. Other photographers soon arrived as flashbulbs illuminated the darkness. Christian Martinez, a French photographer, began snapping shots inside the Mercedes, prompting his rival Rat to yell at him to stop photographing such a horrific event. Martinez cursed Rat and then cried, "Get out of the way! I have the same job as you!"

The vehicle was crushed. The roof had been smashed to seat level, and the grille had been smashed two-thirds of the way back into the dashboard. When French physician Frederick Mailliez saw the accident, he quickly dialed 911 from his car phone. He ran to Diana, 36, who was unconscious at the time. Mailliez was surrounded by a dozen photographers who had assembled to photograph the situation, but none of them attempted to assist. A police officer intervened to save a single paparazzo who was being pummeled by enraged bystanders. The princess was extracted from the debris after two hours, and she was transported to Pitie Salpetriere Hospital, where physicians worked for two hours in vain to save her life. Diana died from cardiac arrest at 4:00 a.m. after suffering severe wounds to her lung, head, and thigh.

The devastating news was met with shock and anguish all throughout the world. Thousands of people flocked to the hospital when Diana's death was announced. French Prime Minister Lionel Jospin was among the first to express regret that the tragedy occurred in his country. "It was so sad that this beautiful young woman, who was loved by everyone and whose every act and gesture was scrutinized, tragically ended her life in France, in Paris," he said. "I wanted to make a gesture because the French were always seduced by her charm."7 Sporting events like professional soccer matches in the United Kingdom were promptly canceled. As incoming Prime Minister Tony Blair spoke for his compatriots, that nation went through a period of terrible mourning. "We are today a nation in Britain in a state of shock, mourning, and grief so deeply painful for us," Blair remarked. "We know how difficult things were for her at times." I'm sure we can only guess. But people all throughout the world, not just in the United Kingdom, remained hopeful about Princess Diana. ...She was the people's princess, and that is how she will remain, in our hearts and memories forever."8 By early am, crowds had gathered outside both her Kensington Palace house and Buckingham Palace. Many people left single bloomers or bouquets. One young girl, no older than three, left a bright yellow, damaged teddy bear. Diana's flag-draped coffin was quickly put into a van outside the hospital for transportation to Villacoublay Airfield and a flight back to London.

Diana, thank you for your time

Diana's coffin was carried in a sad 105-minute procession from Kensington Palace gates to the heart of London. It ultimately made its way to Westminster Abbey, where British monarchs are traditionally interred. More than a million people lined the streets, the largest crowd in that country since a far more joyous occasion in 1945—the German surrender that marked the end of World War II. The procession included Prince Charles, sons William and Harry, the Duke of Edinburgh, and Diana's brother Charles Spencer. Elton John, the pop musician, elicited an outpouring of passion and a torrent of tears by performing a sorrowful rendition of "Candle in the Wind," originally penned for Marilyn Monroe, on the piano. The revised words of the song began, "Goodbye, England's Rose." The centerpiece of the burial, which was displayed on two giant screens in Hyde Park, was Diana's brother's angry yet eloquent and moving eulogy. He called the princess "the most hunted person of the modern age" and the paparazzi "at the opposite end of the moral spectrum" from his sister.

The paparazzi's antics were heavily criticized in the days following the burial, which was observed by an estimated 2.5 billion television viewers in 187 countries. Soon after the accident, Steve Coz, editor of the National Enquirer, said that photographers who photographed the death scene were hoping to make up to $1 million. Coz also mentioned that the tabloids were bidding for the first photograph of Dodi and the princess kissing. "To a paparazzo," Coz explained, "that's like waving a lottery ticket." This was a disaster just waiting to happen."

Yes, that was tragic. Others, though, argued that such a calamity could have been avoided if Diana had taken a firmer stance against the paparazzi years earlier. Daily Mirror reporter James Whitaker, who acknowledged crying as he wrote his story about her death, was among some who felt the princess had used media people, even those as murky as the paparazzi who followed her, for far too long and for her personal profit. Whitaker cited a recent vacation to the French Riviera with Dodi as an example. "She walked on the beach, got on a jet ski, got on a motorboat," Whitaker said. "Why should she not do this?" I'm not saying she can't. But it took a virtuoso performance for us to acquire pictures and a story. It's horrible what happened, but there was an aspect of using the paparazzi and photographers in general to Diana's advantage."

Though the controversy over the paparazzi raged on, tests revealed that driver Henri Paul was legally drunk, shifting the blame. Paul's blood alcohol level was three times the legal limit, and he had ingested the alcohol while also taking Tiapride and the antidepressant Prozac, both of which have specific cautions against combining with alcohol. The circumstances surrounding the accident were important to many people in Britain, but they were even more important to 15-year-old William and 12-year-old Harry, who were on vacation with their father in Scotland when the story broke. They only knew that their mother had died. Diana's boys held back their tears as they walked behind her coffin as it made its way to Westminster Abbey, one of three wreaths that rested on her casket simply read, "Mummy." William appeared particularly distressed. Diana regarded him as more than just a son, but also as a confidant and friend.

Charles had been tasked with informing his sons that their mother had died. After hearing the news, the bereaved prince went for a walk around Balmoral by himself. He experienced a wide range of emotions, including guilt. Perhaps the marriage might have continued if he hadn't been unfaithful, and Diana would not have felt the need to seek comfort in the arms of other men. Charles was especially preoccupied with the impact her death would have on William and Harry, to whom he delivered the devastating news. William had confronted his mother about what he saw as an unhealthy relationship with Dodi; now he would never have the chance to apologize. Harry was overcome with melancholy and a sense of bereavement. He would never again feel the warmth and satisfaction of curling up on the couch with his mum and watching films.

And, sadly, Diana would never again deliver her enchantment to the billions who needed it the most. Hundreds of people representing the organizations she supported joined the somber march as the princess's remains were carried to Westminster Abbey. It was no longer a regal ritual; it was an emotional demonstration of Diana's immense value to the world. People with AIDS, landmine survivors, and homeless advocates all walked to show their support for Diana.

There was a lot to like. The small girl who cared for her pets had grown into a woman who cared for the entire planet.

Epilogue

As the months and years passed, both ludicrous and legitimate conspiracy ideas made their way into the mainstream media. At one point, over 35,000 Web sites were dedicated to generally frivolous theories alleging Di-ana's death was pre-planned. Bitter Mohamed Al-Fayed claimed that Prince Philip murdered the princess because she was about to marry an Egyptian Muslim, who would then become the heir to the throne's half brother. "Prince Philip is the one responsible for giving the order [to have Diana killed]," Al-Fayed stated. "He is extremely racist." He has German ancestors, and I'm convinced he sympathizes with the Nazis."

Every examination into the crash determined that Al-Fayed's claims were false. A three-year investigation led by former Metropolitan Police Commissioner Lord Stevens, nicknamed Operation Paget, ended in the dismissal of every claim made by Al-Fayed and the media. French officials conducted research and came to the same conclusion. Among the claims were that someone shone a light in Paul's eyes to blind him while he was driving, that the royal family wanted Diana dead because she was pregnant with Dodi's child, and that a driver in a Fiat Uno intentionally sideswiped the Mercedes to cause an accident. Le Van Thanh, a Vietnamese plumber, drove the Fiat Uno. He did repaint his automobile red after the collision, but only to avoid prosecution under French law, which makes leaving the site of an accident criminal even if you are not engaged.

While the majority of the British and global public either lost interest in the case or simply accepted Diana's death as an accident, Al-Fayed maintained that Prince Philip ordered the murders of the princess and his son and had British security operatives carry them out. What appeared to be Al-Fayed's last chance to get his idea proven was carried out just after the accident's tenth anniversary in late 2007. In early October, Lord Justice Scott Baker, who was serving as coroner in the case, sought a jury to decide the cause of death. Despite the fact that no one could be named in the case, the jury of six women and five men had the authority to find that it was a murder plot. That situation, though, appeared to be highly improbable. Al-Fayed was disappointed that neither Queen Elizabeth II nor Prince Charles were scheduled to testify, since he believed their knowledge would support his case. Fayed even expanded his argument to include Diana and Dodi announcing their engagement on September 1, the day following the disaster.

Life, on the other hand, moves on. Following Princess Diana's death, Charles requested that the media respect the privacy of his boys, William and Harry. He thought that the same tabloids that played a role in their mother's death would allow the princes to grieve privately and focus on their education without much attention.

William, who is second in line to the throne after his father, excelled in a variety of disciplines at Eton College, including geography, biology, and art history, before taking a year off to visit Chile, work on British dairy farms, and travel Africa. He subsequently went on to study geography at St. Andrews University in Scotland, where he graduated in 2005. Soon after, he enrolled as an officer cadet at the Royal Military Academy Sandhurst and was commissioned as an army officer. He swiftly became a second lieutenant in the Household Cavalry.

Harry's life has become more contentious after the accident that took his mother away. In 1998, he followed William to Eton and traveled to Australia, Argentina, and Africa. During his final tour, he produced a well-received documentary about the plight of orphans in Lesotho. When Harry donned a swastika armband to a costume party in January 2005, he received quite the opposite reaction. The 20-year-old prince apologized sincerely for what he called a bad decision. The incident generated quite a commotion, but it gradually died down when it became clear that it had nothing to do with his political views. Following in his brother's footsteps, Harry enrolled in the Royal Military Academy Sandhurst and spent over a year training as an officer cadet. In 2006, he was also commissioned as a second lieutenant in the Household Cavalry.

Neither son, however, has emotionally separated himself from Diana. In fact, to commemorate the tenth anniversary of her death, William and Harry organized a commemorative memorial performance in her honor. The event was aired in 140 countries, reaching 500 million people. In December 2006, around 22,500 tickets were made available for the concert, which sold out in 17 minutes. The July 2007 performance at Wembley Stadium drew 63,000 people, including Elton John, Sir Tom Jones, Duran Duran, Andrea Bocelli, Rod Stewart, and Kanye West. Speeches by both princes, as well as previous and present world leaders such as Bill Clinton, Nelson Mandela, and Tony Blair, capped off the celebrations, which reached a climax when a video homage to Diana was screened.

Prince Charles was one star who did not attend the concert. Many people in the United Kingdom still saw him as a villain ten years after Diana's murder, claiming that if he had given all of his attention to his wife rather than Camilla, the princess would not have felt the need to seek love elsewhere and would still be alive. Following the death of their mother, Charles reinforced his bond with William and Harry. They accompanied him on various journeys both within the United Kingdom and abroad.

After the catastrophe, Charles' affections for Camilla did not fade. On April 9, 2005, the couple married in a civil ceremony in Windsor. Camilla took the title of Her Royal Highness, the Duchess of Cornwall after her wedding, which was attended by 800 guests and was followed by a reception thrown by the queen. The pair visited the United States in 2005, the Middle East and Western Asia in 2006, and both the United States and the Middle East in 2007. The visits had a very different taste and ambience than those made by Charles and Diana, especially in the last few years of their marriage. The insults and petty fighting that ruined Prince Charles and Princess Diana's public engagements were replaced by the respect the new royal couple had for each other, and the adoring crowds who surrounded Diana wherever she went were replaced by a quieter existence. However, Diana, Princess of Wales' legacy lives on as her kids and those who knew her maintain her memory alive.

Diana, Princess of Wales: A Timeline of Events

1 July 1961 Diana Frances Spencer was born in Norfolk, England.

1967 Summer: Parents Johnnie and Frances separate.

December Diana is enrolled at Silfield Day School after John-nie wins custody of her and her brother Charles.

1969 The divorce of parents Johnnie and Frances becomes official.

1970 Diana is sent to Riddlesworth Hall, a prep school in Norfolk.

1973 Diana continues her education at West Heath School in Kent.

1974 Diana moves with her father and siblings to the family estate in Althorp.

14 July 1976 Much to the dismay of Diana and her siblings, John-nie marries Raine Legge, daughter of romance nov-elist Barbara Cartland.

1977 Diana leaves West Heath, but Johnnie sends her to a Swiss finishing school, which she attends for only a few months.

Diana meets Prince Charles through her sister Sarah.

1979 Diana moves to London with three roommates in an apartment bought by her parents. She assumes work as a housekeeper, nanny, and kindergarten teacher's aide.

1980 Charles begins dating Diana.

3 February 1981 The prince asks Diana to marry him during a dinner at Buckingham Palace.

29 July The wedding of Prince Charles and Diana Spencer is broadcast throughout the world.

5 November It is officially announced that Diana is pregnant.

21 June 1982 Prince William is born.

March 1983 Diana and Charles tour Australia and New Zealand.

Her immense popularity becomes apparent.

15 September 1984 Prince Harry was born.

1988 A conversation with old friend Carolyn Bartholomew convinces Diana to combat her bulimia.

1989 Diana visits Harlem Hospital and Henry Street in New York, showing compassion for the sick, the homeless, and the battered women.

3 June 1991 Prince William is hit in the head with a golf club and suffers a skull fracture. Diana remains by his side while Charles attends a royal engagement, for which he is later criticized.

19 March 1992 Father Johnnie dies of a heart attack.

June Andrew Morton's biography, *Diana, Her True Story,* is published. Diana's struggles with Charles, bulimia, and depression are revealed.

9 December Buckingham Palace announces the official separa-tion of Charles and Diana.

1994 An interview with Jonathan Dimbleby reveals that Charles has had a long love affair with Camilla Parker Bowles. He admits to having seen his mis-tress since 1986.

20 November 1995 A television interview of Diana by journalist Mar-tin Bashir draws an audience of over 20 million viewers.

28 August 1996 Diana and Charles are officially divorced.

January 1997 Diana travels to Africa and launches her campaign

against anti personnel landmines.

July Tabloid photos surface of Diana on a yacht in the French Riviera with new boyfriend Dodi Al-Fayed.

August Diana travels to Bosnia to continue her campaign against anti land mines.

31 August Diana, Al-Fayed, and driver Henri Paul are killed in a car crash as they speed through a Paris tunnel in an attempt to shed paparazzi.

6 September The funeral of Princess Diana attracts millions. Di-ana's body is transported from Westminster Abbey and is buried on an island on the Althorp estate.

Printed in Great Britain
by Amazon

32042851R00089